W9-CLV-532

MR. RIGHT

MR. RIGHT

by
Carolyn Banks

a SECOND CHANCE PRESS book
from
THE PERMANENT PRESS
Sag Harbor, New York 11963

First published 1979 by The Viking Press
Republished January, 1999, by Second Chance Press

Library of Congress Cataloging in Publication Data

Banks, Carolyn.
  Mr. Right / by Carolyn Banks
      p.   cm.
   ISBN 0-933256-91-4
   I.   Title
PS3552. A485M77   1999
813'.54—dc21
                           98-34202
                              CIP

Manufactured in the United States of America

SECOND CHANCE PRESS
4170 Noyac Road
Sag Harbor, NY 11963

SECOND CHANCES

Mr. Right after Twenty Years

Even though I was in my thirties and ought to have known better, I began writing *Mr. Right* with an odd kind of innocence. Lida, my heroine, was a victim of sexual freedom, a woman who had more or less burned out on it. The opening scene, to me, was a comic representation of this.

It never, for a moment—and this is what I mean when I say my 'odd' innocence—occurred to me that the scene would trouble anyone. Imagine my surprise when my editor, Amanda Vaill, told me that the printer, at least initially, had refused to set the opening scene in type.

I laughed with Amanda about this, but at the same time, thought the publisher must have sent my book to some sort of genetic throwback.

Little did I know.

The thing about *Mr. Right* is that it *starts* with a sex scene. There are plenty of steamier scenes in other books, but with *Mr. Right*, you are socked in the face with sex the minute you crack the cover.

But of course, that's what I wanted. I wanted everyone to know how anerotic things had become for Lida. I mean, we can't exactly envy the sex we see her having, can we?

But you know what we do in bookstores; we open the book and start reading. Sometimes our friends read over our shoulders. For this reason, whatever their intended purpose, sex scenes should be placed well into the book. I know that now.

There's some evidence to suggest that, if I'd paid attention, I might have known it back then. My son certainly did.

The very day my agent phoned to say she'd sold *Mr. Right*, my son and I had to go to the laundromat. I guess I was pretty happy and another customer, an old man, noticed and asked what had put me in such a wonderful mood.

"I just sold my first novel," I crowed.

"Oh, really," he said. "I think you can tell a lot about a book from its first sentence. What's yours?"

From way across the room, my son, age thirteen or so, stopped folding towels and came a-running. "Mom, no!" he bellowed, "Don't!"

A lot of men did not laugh at the opening scene. A lot of men want to be seen as conquistadors. These are generally not men I especially like. On the other hand, when I read the scene aloud to a group of female octogenarians who called themselves "The Thinking Cap," they did laugh, a little. That delighted me, proving that we've all been there, all engaged in sexual situations that turned out, shall we say, less-than-storybook? It's the people who can admit that, and laugh at it, that I tend to gravitate toward. *Mr. Right*, then, became a quick way I could sort people out.

The sex in *Mr. Right* got better for the characters as the book went on. A few men—some the husbands of friends of mine, yet—got goofy about it. I remember one such sidling up to me, breathing as if he were a lifelong asthmatic, asking, "Do you write the sex scenes you've lived or the sex scenes you'd like to live?" I guess if I'd said the latter, he'd have hurled me to the tundra and had his way with me right then and there.

The answer to his question, however, is neither. I write the sex scenes my characters have had/are having. Sorry about that. The Negative Capability defense.

But when I was writing *Mr. Right*, I worked especially hard on the sex scenes. I wanted them to be written without the euphemisms of romance novels, but I didn't want them to be what I would label pornographic. I started on Diana's early-on scene, the one where she's imagining her lover, Lou, and what she'd like to do to him. In fact, I was working on that scene so continuously that for a long time I carried it with me in my purse so that I could touch it up from time to time even though I wasn't at home in front of my typewriter.

I mention this because I was putting something in the trunk of my car, my purse slung over my shoulder, when some punk grabbed the purse, yanked, and ran.

About a block away, the police found the purse and everything was still in it—money, credit cards, keys. The only thing missing was the scene. The perp probably still has that typewritten sheet, stained, worn through at the creases.

There's a lot of cross-genre stuff now, but when *Mr. Right* was in manuscript, I kept running into, "What is this? Is it a women's book? Is it a mystery?" That's how the subtitle was born. I don't even know the name of the very funny person who said it, "It's a smartass parafeminist psycho-erotic thriller," but that's what *Mr. Right* became. And you can tell that times have really changed, because now it can be that officially, with those words right smack on the cover.

Mr. Right, to me, is also the sort of book that only an English major would write. There are a lot of literary references and jokes. The one I was especially proud of is a pretty embarrassing example of, as we used to say, where my head was at.

Diana is at a meeting and she thinks of the first line of Ezra Pound's "The Encounter," as a kind of clue. Then she notices Allen, and she is *"feeling his eyes, yes, exploring.*

And when she arose to go..."

The line break cuts to the cafeteria and we pick up with *"She snatched up a napkin and an array of silver."*

Well, of course, I and three other people in the Western hemisphere knew the delicate little poem to which I was paying homage. Here it is, entire:

> *All the while they were talking the new morality*
> *Her eyes explored me.*
> *And when I arose to go*
> *Her fingers were like the tissue*
> *Of a Japanese paper napkin.*

I thought I was being so smart, so clever, so *literary*. I loved the way Diana's snatching up of the napkin kind of reversed the effect of the napkin in Pound's poem. I probably imagined some bespectacled scholar abandoning James Joyce's work in favor of mine. It sort of touches me now, to have thought this kind of thing meaningful or important.

My favorite scene—a scene that didn't wear off on me—is one between Diana, Lida and Eddie, one of Diana's sons. Eddie, the little weasel, is doing the dishes and he whines that can't get one of the pots clean. Diana, being supermom, is about to tell him she'll do it, but Lida butts in and tells him to throw the pot away. That scene still makes me laugh.

One penultimate thing. Last year I was grooming a horse who spooked and slammed into me, breaking my nose. There's a character in *Mr. Right* whose nose is broken and when it happens, she says that her nose doesn't hurt. "It just feels big," she announces.

I thought of that character's line on my way to the hospital. I felt triumphant, because *just big* was exactly how my broken nose felt, something I hadn't known for sure when I wrote the scene twenty years before.

Finally, like all good authors, I sent a copy of *Mr. Right* to my mom as soon as I had the finished book in my hands. She didn't reply, so I figured she hated it and was just being her version of tactful. Three years later she wrote a letter that began, "Your grandmother was taken to the hospital and while I was sitting in the waiting room, I finally had a chance to look at your book. All I can say is, I'm glad your father didn't live to see this." Et cetera.

Marty and Judy Shepard of Second Chance Press approached me about reprinting *Mr. Right* when it first came out. I'm very grateful that they didn't forget. I'm proud to have written *Mr. Right*, proud to have my book out there again for all the world— my mother notwithstanding—to see.

Carolyn Banks
Bastrop, Texas

MR. RIGHT

1

Lida watched him unroll the thing along his penis much as she had watched her father wallpaper the kitchen. He left a gap of about two inches at the top. Her father, she recalled, had been more precise.

"Why does it look like that?" She chose these words in favor of, "Asshole, you don't have it on right."

"That's where the semen goes," Charles said patiently.

"There isn't that much semen," she argued.

"Look, Lida, I know how to do this."

Except that no bell bobbed from the tip, it looked like a fool's cap. A puppet wearing a fool's cap. She didn't say it. Instead, she inserted the plastic tube into her vagina. "Yuck," she told him, "it's like stuffing yourself with a jar of cold cream."

They both sighed deeply.

"I really don't feel like fucking," she said.

"Well, I do." He reached for her purposefully.

The rubber-coated sheath cut through the gel. "It's like having an internal," she announced as he heaved back and forth.

"Will you shut up?" he said.

"No, I mean it," she kept on, "it's awful, it's like . . ."

He withdrew before she could come up with a new analogy. "God damn you." He sat up. "God damn you!"

She looked at his penis and saw that it was clean and dry to the base. Beyond that, his pubic hair was coated with what looked like lard. "When did you take it off?" she asked.

"Take what off?"

"The rubber."

"I didn't," he said, looking down at himself. "Oh, shit." He began to feel around the bed. "I think it's still, uh . . . " He looked at her uneasily.

"You're kidding."

"No, I'm not."

"It couldn't be."

"It has to be."

She leaned back and felt inside herself. "It's not there," she said.

"Go all the way up."

"Thank God I'm thirty-five," she recited, probing as she spoke, "and not a virgin." She pulled it out and set it on the pillow.

They both stared at it.

No one who knew Lida casually would have called her a romantic. Lida, by her own reckoning, had slept with thirty men. She had, in fact, compiled a written list of names in her friend Diana's living room one night. "But," she had told Diana then, "I've only been promiscuous, oh, maybe three or four times."

"I fear," Diana had said, "for the safety of my sons."

"Not yet." Lida had laughed. "But maybe next year."

Now she sat in Diana's kitchen, depressed. "It's relentless," she said, "and I hate it."

"It could be worse." Diana's voice was reassuring, like a flat-handed pat. "Believe me, it could be worse."

"How would *you* know?" Lida was sometimes brutal.

Marriage had been Diana's introduction to sex. And for the twelve years since her divorce, Diana had lived a celibate life, in part because she thought her role as materfamilias demanded it, in part because she was a Jane Austen specialist.

"My life is relentless, too, in its own way," Diana said. She thought of Lida explaining the device of apostrophe to an office-full of students at the small community college—largely attended by black inner-city late-adolescents—where they both taught. " 'O ramrod of rectitude!' " Lida had shouted, her arm sweeping in Diana's direction. The students had giggled. "I'm tired," Diana said now, her voice tight, "of being that 'ramrod of rectitude.' Really tired."

"Oh, shit."Lida sighed. "That really got to you. Oh, shit."

"Well, sure it got to me. It's true."

"I thought you wanted it that way."

"That's what everyone thinks," Diana said. And now that it was half out, she thought that she would say it all. "But it infuriates me that you would think so, too."

"Then change it," Lida challenged. "Damn!" She slapped her hand against the table. "Change it! Go get yourself laid."

"Lida," she said, "can't you see that I will never 'get myself laid'?" She shook her head, just thinking of it. "Never! I might get up the nerve to join Parents Without Partners or something . . . " She watched the I'm-Going-to-Be-Sick expression that Lida donned. "Okay, maybe I could join Mensa. But the point is"—she grew serious again, though

3

Lida was still making faces—"I'm nothing like you. I will *never* get myself laid."

"At least," Lida said, "I'll know what to put on your tombstone."

"Oh, I'm sorry I brought it up." Diana walked to the sink and filled a pot with water. She lit the range and put the pot down on the burner so hard that the water sloshed over the sides and sizzled.

"I'm no good at solving other people's problems," Lida tried to explain. "You tell me, more or less, that you'd like to—I don't know—have someone around. But then you won't do anything about it."

"Do?" Diana walked back toward the table. "Do? I don't know what to do. I'm forty-three years old. What do I do? What do *you* do?"

"I don't do anything."

"Well, you must. Something I've never been able to do. You must! Thirty men didn't just come crawling out of the woodwork. I would like to, just once, try *your* kind of relentless. I've had my kind up to here."

Lida sat toying with a strand of her impeccably silky black hair. Finally she shoved her chair back, sighed dramatically, and stood up. "Hey, are you making coffee?"

"Yes," said Diana briefly.

Lida walked over to the refrigerator, opened the door, and stared inside.

"What are you looking for?" Diana asked.

"I wish I knew. Someone who isn't a . . . hey, what's this?" She pulled forth a small waxed container of half-and-half. "What are you, having a party?" She cocked her head, lifted her brows.

"No," said Diana, busy with the coffeepot. "I wish you'd sit down."

"What? Are you mad at me?"

"Yes, I'm mad. I'm mad because I'm disappointed. We talk about something that matters, and then we stop talking

4

about it. And nothing changes."

"What can I do? What can I say that will change it? You want me to do a number on you? Okay. You look like shit, Diana. You dress like shit. You wear those cat-eye glasses that my mother wouldn't even wear and you pile your hair on your head like some archetypal librarian. You have a mustache. Jesus Christ, Diana! You have a mustache! And you're asking me why no one ever makes a pass at you?"

"I'm not talking about passes," Diana said, feeling battered.

"Oh, no? Then what are you talking about? What's relentless? Crawling into an empty bed every night, right? Isn't that what you're saying? Come on, isn't it?" But now it was Lida who began to cry. She rummaged in her purse and came up with a handful of Kleenex.

"I'm not sure I know what's going on here," Diana said, running her finger along her upper lip.

Lida sniffed and sniveled. "I'm not trying to make it sound like some magazine makeover." She blew her nose. "But you don't have anyone because you look as though you don't want anyone. And I'm crying because I don't have anyone..."

Diana moved to interrupt, but Lida held up her hand. "No, don't argue. I don't have anyone for very *long*—and I never have, Diana—no matter how I look. Your problem is simple. The electrolysis lady at Garfinckel's could solve your problem. My problem can't be solved. My problem is me."

And then they were talking about Lida again. Wasn't that always the way? Wasn't that what drew people to her and what drove them away? Lida knew it. She had pasted on her office wall an old *New Yorker* cartoon—a peacock whose tail reached the full width of the page. "And now," the bird addressed its puny and plain companion, "let's talk about *you.*"

"Shit," Lida said now. "I don't want to talk about my problems. I really don't. How does it always happen?"

"It's not your *fault*," Diana said.

Lida was looking in her purse for her makeup. "I refuse to believe it was the abortion," she said. "I hated his guts long before then." She frowned, remembering the little reefs of hatred that had signaled the mainland. "Bone dry," she said. "That's the way I feel right now. Bone dry."

"Temporary," Diana assured her.

"It damn well better be. Otherwise, when I go into the hospital—"

"The hospital!"

Lida sipped at her coffee now, all passion spent. "I didn't tell you?"

"No, you didn't tell me."

"I'm having my tubes tied." Lida shrugged. "I mean, just in case you're right and this feeling *is* temporary."

"You're being sterilized?"

"Why not? I don't want to go through *this* again."

Diana was relieved, laughing. "I'll bring you a novel," she said.

"I'll just be in overnight," Lida told her. "Maybe not even that."

"I'll bring you one anyway. Something with a lot of lust and miscegenation."

"Oh, God," Lida said. "Lust, yes, but please, skip the miscegenation. Just bring me a mystery."

"A carefully considered choice." Diana handed the book to Lida. "I just knew you'd love the cover."

Lida looked at it and guffawed. The photo showed a man in black sitting cross-legged in a chair. The gun in his hand, lengthened by a silencer, was obviously intended to represent his penis.

"Some lovelorn designer's idea of subtlety," Lida said. "But, oh, God, ain't it the truth?" She looked at Diana. "Have you read it?"

"Are you kidding? With a cover like that?"

"Well, at the moment, it beats curling up with the *Areopagitica*." Lida's Milton course was scheduled for the fall semester. "Lord, Diana, did you ever hear them pronounce *Areopagitica*?"

Diana cast an uneasy glance at the black woman in the bed next to Lida's. "Call you tomorrow"—she eased toward the door—"when you're home."

Lida, who had already begun to plumb the book's pages, didn't speak. She gave a perfunctory wave that was intended to serve as both thank you and good-bye.

❧

"Oh, Jesus, you've got to read this, Diana." Lida burst into Diana's office brandishing the book. "No kidding, this guy is better than Milton. Better, even, than Jane Austen." She laughed at her own exaggeration, then topped it. "No, really," she said.

Diana gestured at the syllabus she was struggling to complete. "I'm sorry," she said, "but the real world beckons."

"Listen . . . " Lida prepared to read from the book. "Just listen to a few lines."

Diana was irritated. Lida always tried to sweep everyone up in her own enthusiasm. She often succeeded, which was, in large measure, the secret of her security on the faculty of Brady State College—that, and the fact that she'd slept with only two of her students, both very discreet young men.

Diana remembered asking Lida, "Were they black?" It seemed a silly question, since almost all of the students were. But Lida had said no. And while Diana was rapidly

7

running the white males on campus by on a sort of mental treadmill, Lida had continued talking.

"One," Lida said, "had skin the color of root beer. Or, if you want to get fancy, Calvados, you know, the brandy? And the other one, his skin was lighter. More like peanut butter."

"They *were* black," Diana said, hastily dismissing the white men who stood uncomfortably in the glare of her mind's eye.

" 'Colored,' " Lida told her, "is really more precise. It really is." And when Diana asked a question that even she, herself, found unthinkable, Lida repaid her. "It was just what you'd expect," she teased. "They didn't wear Jockey shorts. They wore zebra-skin loincloths. And when they kissed me, my lips just bled and bled."

"Tell me," Diana had insisted.

"It wasn't that great. But I think it was an age thing, not a race thing. God, I hope it was an age thing."

"Who were they?"

"I can't believe this, Diana, what is *with* you?" But then she answered. "One was back before you came. His name was George Washington. I mean, how could I resist?"

"You slept with him because of his name?"

"Oh, God, no. Now, that's what I mean by promiscuous. No. I slept with him because of his sense of humor. He said, 'Don' you wanna put a little sign right up over yo' bed tellin' folks George Washington slept here?' " Lida had laughed, as much at her memory as at the way Diana seemed to shrink in the face of it. "See?" she had said. "I can see a line like that would never get to you. But it really got to me."

Now she sat at Diana's table reading the lines that were getting to her today, but Diana pretended not to hear. "Come on, Diana," Lida said, "you have to admit that he's damn good. In fact, he's fantastic. In fact, I'm in love."

"Who is he?" Diana relented.

8

"I don't know." Lida flipped the cover shut and read the author's name. "It just says 'Duvivier.' That's a strange name." She read the back cover and the inside flaps and the copyright notice. "That's all, just 'Duvivier.' "

"Leave it," Diana said, "I'll get to it."

2

Duvivier. He had seen the name on a brass plate under some painting or other. It had the quality of an infinitive, he thought. Yes. To revive. The fact that the name meant nothing of the sort did not intrude upon the sense of irony that he felt. He chose it, smiling.

But Duvivier was merely one of his names. The three under which he wrote included those of Paul Philippe Grisone and Jackson R.W. Bishop. His checks arrived and were deposited in the Bishop name. His fourth name, he assumed, had long been forgotten.

He heard the scrape of the milk cans on the pavement and the sound of the cart moving off. It was later than the light had led him to believe. He walked to the window, pushed back the curtain, and looked down into the street.

A gray day, a day that the tourists would complain about. The Ministry of Tourism routed them through the village regularly now that the restoration of the town was almost complete. He would leave Pedraza for good, he decided.

He had come here many years earlier. The water was sweet and the air was thin and few in the village could muster more than an English phrase or two. It had taken a half day by Land Rover to make the climb, and that, too, swayed him. There was nothing in Pedraza save what he, in one of his novels, had called an amniotic solitude.

Which novel? He could not remember. Nonetheless, it was a good line, a bright line. No matter how easily the words came, he would still entertain himself now and again by recalling those of his phrases he most admired. Only occasionally, say, on one of his infrequent trips to America, would he widen his audience, parading before his companions the very excellent and tested dialogue of one of his characters.

But his characters were not enough. He had created their authors as well.

Duvivier, for instance, was the least serious and most successful of the lot. He was a bit splashy, perhaps, given to bullying waiters and carrying enormous sums of cash. If he chose to sleep with a woman, it would be as Duvivier, who had a talent for gymnastic sex and who was not averse to impertinent coversation.

And were he to sleep with a man, he would be Paul Philippe Grisone, prone to exoticism and languor.

Jackson R.W. Bishop, though not yet fifty, was, alas, a crusty celibate.

"Señor Beeshop."

"Si?"

"El correo." The maid had brought his mail.

He instructed her to set it on the table in the hall. Even his Spanish was more fluent than was necessary here. He would definitely leave Pedraza.

He opened the packet from New York first. It was a scattering of reviews of the latest Duvivier book, the seventh to appear in the States. He read them, though he already knew what they would contain. His American audience saw how well he used the form, and missed, utterly, how brilliantly he mocked it. But even half-read, Duvivier made such a lot of money.

Jackson R.W. Bishop went down to breakfast.

3

"Is this the end of the line?" The newly sterilized Lida had circled three-fourths of the block surrounding the movie house.

"I think so," he said.

"Jesus"—Lida shook her head—"I expected to find the Holy Grail."

They laughed, and then, as strangers do, lapsed into silence. Lida stared at her feet, wondering if the tennis shoes she was wearing made her look like a housewife.

"Are you a lesbian?" he asked.

"Why? Do they wear tennis shoes?"

The line advanced until they rounded the corner nearest the entrance. It stopped, then it began to dissolve. "Sold out," a man called, "next show, eleven-fifty-five."

"By eleven-fifty-five"—Lida looked at her watch—"I'll be . . ."

"Great idea!" He offered his arm.

"Where the hell are you taking me?" Lida asked. "To Baltimore?"

He had driven out Connecticut Avenue to the Beltway, a circumferential highway that feeds the Washington suburbs. "I'm taking you to my office." He offered a reassuring smile.

"Oh, married, huh?" She rolled the window down and let the night air in. "I should have known."

"Does it make a difference?" He looked over at her briefly.

"That's a corny line. An easy lay is an easy lay is an easy lay."

He frowned over the steering wheel, guiding the car to the exit ramp.

"In case you're wondering," Lida said, "I'm an old-maid English teacher. That's why I talk this way."

"I *was* wondering, as a matter of fact."

He drove around a flat red building and parked in the empty lot. They advanced to the back door under a streetlamp. He fished for another set of keys, opened the lock, and switched on the light.

The hallway was dingy and uninspired. "If I had an office like this," Lida said, "I'm not sure I'd bring anyone to it."

He led her to yet another door, repeated the procedure, and stepped aside.

Lida preceded him into the room. "Much better," she said.

"We aren't there yet." There was one more door. "Wait." He went inside and lit a small table lamp.

Lida sat on the sofa and stared at the row of diplomas that faced her. "Oh, no. Not a doctor."

He laughed. "Psychiatrist," he said, laughing still.

"Did someone I know put you up to this?"

He began to undo the knot in his tie.

14

4

Jackson R.W. Bishop reminded Duvivier that he had contracted to produce still another book.

Duvivier weakened, agreeing that it was wise to commit to paper the first of the violent deaths that would send the new volume skittering up the charts.

He undressed, snatched a towel from the rack in the bathroom, and leaned back against the mattress. The night air was cold. He would connect the heater later, after he had worked. It would be a kind of reward.

He smiled, stroking his genitals with his left hand. The fingers of that hand, since the difficulty in America, would not close. When his penis was erect, he began a steady rhythm with the right.

The eyes of his victim widened, suddenly aware. His hand moved faster. What was it that he felt, that first sensation? Semen spilled across his fingers onto his legs. Yes. Warm blood on his cold hands. How had he known she was dead? The way she had fallen.

Done.

He toweled himself, then sat naked at the typewriter to lock the scene into words.

5

Lida was drinking iced tea from one of the hundreds of jelly glasses Diana kept in her cupboard. "It's like one of those made-for-teevee movies," she said, stirring noisily. "His wife is rotting with cancer and his oldest daughter is off at Bennington majoring in something called Contact Improvisation."

"Wasn't that your major?"

"For real, kiddo. And the other kids, they ride horses. Isn't that a gas?" Lida had learned all that she knew about horses from the poetry of Robinson Jeffers; she therefore thought it an unsavory pastime.

"Is there anything else I have to know about this man?"

"Yeah. He fakes his orgasms."

"What would you expect from a psychiatrist?" Diana lifted Lida's glass and ran a damp cloth over the table where it had rested. She carried the spoon to the sink, came back, and wiped the spot where the spoon had been as well.

"Why don't you sit down?" Lida was annoyed.

"No, I've got to get this stuff done." Diana emptied the ashtray into a paper bag, then wiped the bowl of it clean. It was the second time since Lida's arrival that she'd done that.

"Why are you fussing around like this?" Lida asked.

"I don't know."

"What is it? What's the matter?"

"Oh, I've got to give a paper. Very near Bennington, in fact."

"When?"

"Oh, not for weeks. Months, in fact."

"*That's* what's the matter?"

"Okay." Diana sat down. She picked the ashtray up and stared at it as though it were a crystal ball. "Lida"—she spoke warily—"I've got to know. Do you have stretch marks?"

"Stretch marks!" Lida's mouth wagged open and her eyes gleamed. "The half-and-half!" she shouted.

"What?"

"The half-and-half. In your refrigerator. I should have guessed."

"Guessed what?"

"Who is he?" Lida asked.

"I didn't say that." Diana laughed.

"Come *on*, who?"

"Someone who comes for coffee," Diana said.

"All this time? That's all he does is come for coffee?"

"So far."

"Ah, but you're ready."

"I think I might be ready."

"When do I get to meet him?"

"Never," Diana said, "you'd make fun of him."

"Why? Does spittle run out of the corners of his mouth? Does he fart in public?"

"Stop this," Diana insisted. "Damn it, Lida, do you or don't you have stretch marks?"

18

"I don't know," Lida said, "what do they look like?"

"Help me," Diana said. "Pay attention, just this once."

"How can I help? Nobody in my life comes for coffee." It was true. "What kind of help?"

"Well, where, for instance."

"What's wrong with here?"

"The kids," Diana said.

"How about a motel?"

"I can't see myself doing that." Diana removed her glasses and rubbed the bridge of her nose. "Besides, he's married. Someone might see."

"Okay, listen. I'll be teaching that presession course pretty soon. Every goddamn day of the week." The Novel of Crime and Detection. Diana had winced at the title. "Unscholarly," she'd sniffed.

Diana looked at Lida now. What did this course have to do with anything?

"So," Lida went on, "bring him to my place. I'll be away all afternoon. And there's no one to see."

"Maybe," Diana said.

Lida's place was a narrow frame house, three stories tall. It had a peaked roof and, in another sense, was peaked overall. It resisted collapse, Diana thought, only to defy its neighbors: the furniture-factory outlet across the street, the taxi stand next door, the betting parlor that shared the yard in the rear.

Lida could have afforded a high-rise, or a town house, or a green-wreathed suburban standard. Why had she chosen that place? And why the town of Laurel, whose only asset was a racetrack to which Lida had never been?

"It's so seamy," Lida boasted. "There isn't a kid for miles. And the touts and tipsters, they never look up from the racing form."

"Maybe," Diana repeated.

"And don't worry about stretch marks. I have those pinky light bulbs. You'll look great. Anyway, I've been meaning to ask, did it hurt?"

"Did what hurt?"

"Garfinckel's. What do they use, little needles?"

Diana smiled. "I didn't think you'd noticed."

"You must think I'm blind. And speaking of blind . . ." She took Diana's glasses off the table and raised them to her own eyes, squinting. "When are you going to get rid of these?"

Diana took them from her, replacing them defiantly.

It was a gesture which Lida ignored. "Okay," she said. "So much for your troubles. Now you can listen to mine."

"You already told me. He fakes his orgasms."

"Not *him*. He's one of the Wrong Men. I'm talking about Duvivier. Ah, Duvivier!" She let her voice caress the name.

"What about him?" Diana reached across the table for Lida's compact mirror. She turned her face this way and that, as if she were considering its purchase.

"I'm in love with him, no shit. I even called his publisher in New York? Seare and Jolly? I talked to this idiot in the publicity department. You should have heard me. She said, 'Look, I'm just a temporary,' like I was giving her a hard time? And I said, 'Honey, aren't we *all*?' Anyway, she laughed and said she'd send me a list of everything he's ever done. The Duvivier canon. I'll tell you . . ." She paused to watch Diana with the mirror. "See? Better, huh?"

Diana grinned.

"I'll tell you," Lida went on. "I'm only teaching that silly presession course so I can read all of his books on company time. And you know the neatest thing about his books?" She tilted the chair backward, as a child might, and dreamily eyed the ceiling. "The neatest thing is that he obviously has such a great time writing them."

20

6

He slipped into his heavy jacket and walked toward the square. A gaggle of tourists stood in front of the church. Two were photographing the clock. It was Pedraza's least photogenic feature.

Americans, clearly. The women shivered in light sweaters over what was sold in the less sultry months as "cruise wear." Americans thought that all of Spain was warm and sunny the year long. The Department of Tourism did little to disabuse them of that notion.

One of the men was telling another about the discomforts with which he had passed the night. Gastric upsets, chills, all of it due to bottled water and the lack of central heating.

The young man listened, nodding throughout the recital. "Exactly," he would say at the end of each sentence. "Exactly."

One of the women wore a black felt beret. He imagined her

in Madrid, thumbing through the phrase book to make its purchase. It undoubtedly made her feel very Spanish, very in tune. She had not noticed that only the old men wore them.

"Here comes a native!" she shrieked, pointing at him with one hand, snatching at her husband's sleeve with the other.

She broke from the others and fell into step beside him. "Can we take your picture?" she asked.

"You don't have to ask him, for God's sake, just *take* it!" the man shouted.

Jackson R.W. Bishop raised his hands so that they obscured his face.

"You're scaring him, Frank," she said. "He doesn't understand and you're scaring him."

"Aw, bullshit." Frank clicked the shutter anyway.

7

Diana could not believe that she had allowed this to happen. She sat in the car wondering how to stop it. Lida was driving too fast and it frightened her. She held onto the bar on the dashboard.

"What will you do with the kids when you're in Vermont?" Lida asked it angrily.

"It's not Vermont. It's New Hampshire."

"I thought you said Bennington."

"I said *near* Bennington."

"Oh." Lida turned into the shopping center. "I need cigarettes," she explained.

All the while Lida was in the drugstore, Diana sat frozen. She wished for the courage to walk away from the car. But she knew she would not. She surveyed the women who walked along the mall, noting their legs, mostly.

In the late-summer sun, most of them wore shorts. Not too

short, of course, but short enough to demonstrate that the exercise of bearing children was not sufficient. There were knotted blue-veined thighs, fat-drappled thighs, thighs with silvery stretch marks.

Lida returned, tearing the cellophane from the package.

"Do you know, Lida," she said, "that I'm eight years older than you are?"

"You told me. So?"

"What I mean is, my kids think of me as old. I don't think they think of you as old."

"They should see my tits sag."

"I'm hoping"—Diana laughed—"that moment can be postponed indefinitely."

"You haven't told me where your kids will be while you're off giving your paper. New Hampshire." Lida started the engine and threw the car into reverse.

"Bill's agreed to take them." Bill was her ex-husband. He lived in Virginia.

"Why can't Bill agree to take them so you can spend time at home with what's-his-face?" It was a fair question. "Don't answer that," Lida said, "I already know."

They turned into the housing development 'and Lida squinted at the street sign. "Relax," she said, "we may never find it."

It was a more depressing tract than most, with wan little homes that the real-estate ads described as "ramblers."

"Jesus Christ," Lida said, "he's not even lower-middle-class."

"I knew you'd make fun of him."

It was the sort of neighborhood where women hung their wash and sullenly compared it to that of their neighbors. Backyards enclosed in Cyclone fences. An occasional motorboat perched on a trailer.

"God," Diana said, "I hope no one's home."

"He's probably paneling the basement," Lida comforted.

"I don't know why I let you talk me into this."

24

"Hey! I couldn't have found this place without you!"

It was true. Bit by bit, Diana had grown curious about what she called the "other half" of his life. In reality, it was more the other nine-tenths. Perhaps even more than that.

One night, when she ought to have been grading essays, she found herself paging through the telephone directory. There it was.

She sat, absurdly, staring at it. She ran her index finger across the line of type, feeling her pulse quicken and her breath come short. Ridiculous. She slammed the book shut and hurriedly replaced it on the counter, relieved that none of her children had come bounding into the room to force her to explain what she was doing.

Now she and Lida were driving past his house.

"It's that one," Lida said, gesturing with her chin.

"For God's sake, keep moving." Diana resisted a histrionic urge to throw herself to the floor of the car.

Lida eased into Diana's driveway and sat with the engine running. "Well," she said, "let me know when you want to go on another reconnaissance mission."

Diana flushed.

"It wasn't so stupid," Lida said, "I've done lots worse."

Diana's smile was thin.

"Look at the bright side," Lida continued. "He didn't have a flamingo in his front yard. Or a little nigger boy with a lantern. Isn't it comforting to know that?"

Diana closed the door to her bedroom behind her. She took her shoes off and placed them, side by side, on the closet floor.

Downstairs, two of her sons were arguing. She hoped she would not be called upon to referee. She heard a scuffle, then

25

glass breaking, then the slam of the screen door. Another slam. They were gone.

She pulled the pillows out from under the spread and propped them up against the headboard. Then she took the Duvivier book from the nightstand where it had accused her lo these weeks. She got into bed and tried to concentrate.

Lida's assessment of the man had been correct. He was, Diana decided, too clever to be read so carelessly. She let the book fall.

She looked across to her desk. The *Oxford English Dictionary* stood to one side of it. One of the volumes had been removed and lay open, as it had since May. She imagined Lou—the obscure object of her desire—flipping through its pages. "What kind of book is this?" he would say. "You need a goddamned microscope to read it."

"It comes with its own magnifying glass," she would tell him.

And he would leave it there, just that way, open to page 701.

By the end of the semester, her desk would be littered with papers. There would be blue books, a stack of them, fastened with a rubber band. And lined sheets torn from spiral-bound pads, the sort with edges that fell like confetti to the carpet. Occasionally there would be crisp white bond, typed and stapled in the corner. And maybe there would be Lou, his belly spilling out over the tops of his trousers, his socks tossed at the foot of her bed.

She thought of that house, imagining the bric-a-brac that filled each room. Did he ever sit, there in that house, and think of her?

That house. And in it, the room he shared with his wife.

She closed her eyes.

She saw herself slipping into their bedroom, thinking it empty. Then she would see him, asleep, naked, a sheet thrown across his body from his waist to his ankles. She would lean against the edge of the bed opposite his and listen to his breathing. She would come to his bed, sit cautiously, afraid, listening for footsteps. She would run her hand over the sheet, over his stomach and his thighs and his penis. Then, under the sheet, along the inside of his leg.

She would hold his testicles soft against the palm of her hand.

She saw him, waking up, smiling, taking the sheet away. She would not be afraid anymore, but would lean down and run the tip of her tongue over his testicles. He would laugh a little. She would lick his penis, her tongue flat and big, hold his penis in her mouth and run her lips stickily up and down and around.

He would touch her hair and the back of her neck and her face. She would look and find him smiling still and she would lick the palm of his hand and he would pull at her to come up toward him.

She would wear a skirt and a blouse. No shoes, no stockings. He would unbutton her blouse and suck at her nipples and lick her breasts and her lips and her neck. She would be dripping wet with wanting him. She would go crazy if he didn't put his penis inside her. But he would, he would, and while he was fucking her, she would feel her nipples brushing his chest and touch his back and his ass and his legs and then his nipples and his shoulders and his hair.

He would come. She would smell it and feel the heat of it inside her. She would have her arms around him, her fingers in his hair. And they would lie there, smiling, damp, soft.

"Mother!" A teenage voice carried up the staircase. "Are you home?"

Lida advanced on the girl in the second row and stood beside her chair, her hands on her hips, her voice shrill. "What do you mean, LaChelle, you haven't *read* it?"

"Well, uh, I, uh . . ."

"Has anyone in here read it?" she demanded of the class,

27

her eyes leaping from one black face to the next. "Leroy?"

Leroy looked away.

"Falsetine?"

Falsetine added to the graffiti on the arm of her chair.

She didn't bother to call on anyone else. So this was presession. In the college catalog, how had it been described? "An intense learning experience designed to introduce the student to the joy of higher learning before he/she must meet its rigor."

Rigor, Lida thought, as in *rigor mortis.* But what could be expected of a college which required only that its students be prehensile?

It was then that Falsetine dropped her pen. "That does it!" Lida walked to the lectern, gathered up her notes, and jammed them into her purse. "Come back tomorrow when you've read it, or don't come back at all."

Lida had long ago stopped awaiting the day when tongues of flame would descend and hover over each fluffy Afro. The wonder was that she'd ever envisioned it at all. What had she been like in those days? Before she'd put her soul on ice?

"Girl, come back here," one of the students called after her. "I don't want no F." She knew his voice. Jame Jackson. Despite the fact that he'd enlisted in this "intense learning experience," he'd not yet begun to affix the final S to his first name. Nor to anything else. Lida remembered his admissions essay, a treatise on *Uncle Tom Cabin.* Nonetheless, Lida's recommendation that he be placed in the remedial group had been cast aside. Jame Jackson was probably an English major.

She bounded down the stairs and into her basement office. She sat at her desk musing. How would she get them to read Milton? Was there a comic-book edition? In blackface? That might work.

Though the door was open, someone knocked on it.

"Go away," Lida said without turning.

The knock came again.

"I mean it." Lida walked to the door. Four of her students

stood there dumbly in the corridor. "Go away." She pushed the door shut.

The phone rang. It was Diana. "Why aren't you in class?" she asked.

"Aw, the fuckers! They didn't even read the material. Can you imagine? They can't even read a simple detective story. I walked out."

Diana thought of the Duvivier and her failure to start it. She said nothing.

"What's up?" Lida asked. "Why did you call if you thought I'd be in class?"

"I was practicing."

"Practicing what?"

"Getting up my nerve," Diana said. She took a deep breath. "Does that offer still hold?" she asked, the words tumbling out, banging into each other, it seemed.

"What offer?" Lida asked.

"You know, your house?"

"Oh, sure. When?"

"Tomorrow?"

"Fine," Lida said. She hung up, even more in a fume. How could Diana think of men at a time like this? Or at all? They were all the same. Hadn't she told Diana just the other day all about her latest lover, the psychiatrist? The only argument in his favor had been the flexibility of his schedule. She thought, now, of their last time. Very last time, she hoped.

"Is there anything I can do to make it better?" After sex he always spoke in the voice that disc jockeys use on FM stations. The voice, she guessed, he assumed with his patients.

"No." She looked over, to find him smiling at the ceiling. Christ, she congratulated herself, would anyone ever guess how kind you can be?

Lida glanced at the clock. Presession classes were three hours long. She had much time to kill. She started across the campus lawn.

Lawn, that was a laugh. It looked more like a sandlot with an

29

occasional tuft of grass. Lida kicked at the tufts whenever she could.

She pushed at the door to the Student Union and it opened with a bang—the whoosher to keep that from happening had long since been stolen.

Several students were inside. Some sat at tables, some leaned against the wall. One sat on the radiator near the window, snapping her fingers and rolling her shoulders to an unheard melody. Word of her classroom outburst, Lida saw, had already spread. There had been loud conversation when she had opened the door. Now there was a cramped silence.

Lida put a dime in the coffee machine and watched the liquid fall into the cup. There were little pockets of laughter behind her. From the corner of her eye she saw someone approach. LaChelle.

She brushed past the girl and placed the cup on the nearest table. "Go away, LaChelle." She took a paperback from her bag. "I'm trying to read."

The others giggled. "Shit," one of them said, drawing the word into two distinct syllables.

Lida flipped the book to the place she had marked, the point at which Duvivier's hero was about to couple with the first of a score of women. She read pointedly until LaChelle backed away.

Gradually, the activity returned to normal. Someone played the jukebox. Someone else broke one of the sugar shakers that graced each table. Curses and loud laughter followed.

Lida read two pages, stopped suddenly, then read the scene again. God damn! She had not been wrong. The lady had just apologized for menstruating and the gentleman had condescended to fuck her anyway! God damn! She had thought of Duvivier as providing respite from the humdrum of her lovers and her life. But now! Even he seemed a traitor.

She remembered Charles, lying naked in that tacky little apartment of his. Earlier, when he'd discovered she was menstruating, he had made his displeasure plain. "When will this be over?" he'd asked.

"Not for a while," she'd said, "since it just started this morning."

"Lida, I am horny as hell," he had said. "Go take that thing out and come to bed."

God damn men. Would a rapist, she wondered, let you take your Tampax out if you asked him?

But Lida had taken it out and gone to Charles.

Somewhere a bell rang to signal a change of classes. Still seething, Lida put her book away and went to get her mail. Well. At least the Seare and Jolly temporary hadn't let her down. Well, well. She took the envelope, unopened, back to her desk.

Should she? Hell. She reeled a sheet of paper into the type-writer. But where would she send her protest?

Care of Seare and Jolly, of course. She had their address, right there on the desk.

"My dear Duvivier," she wrote, her fingers like hammers on the keys.

8

"Why are we going to this?" Diana asked, her question warring against the sound of Lida's front tires rubbing the curb.

"Because"—Lida looked into the rearview mirror and scraped into reverse—"they have a pool."

"I didn't bring my suit," Diana said.

"Oh, you didn't know?" She cut the engine off and looked at Diana with mock amazement. "The Feltons swim naked."

A fully clothed and immensely pregnant Lucille Felton came out of the house and greeted them. "Oh, you're already laughing," she said, as though she didn't quite approve. "Well, did you bring your suits?"

Lida held up a handful of green bouclé.

"Good! Come on inside!" Lucille waved them in with a flabby arm.

"Can you believe that body?" Lida said *sotto voce*. "And she's in her twenties."

"Lida," Diana defended, "she's pregnant."

"I'm not talking about her belly. I'm talking about her arms."

"First," Lucille was saying, "I want to show off my latest treasure." She led them into a freshly painted alcove. "There!" she said, stepping to one side with overweight grace.

"It's lovely!" Diana said.

"Yes . . . " Lucille picked up a little porcelain vase and hugged it. "Doesn't it have the dearest shape? I got it for the bathroom, but Jerry thought it worked much better out here. Said it got in his way when he shaved or something. What is it, honey?" She finally took notice of her son, who had been standing patiently beside her.

"What's that?" the boy said, pointing at the bathing suit that Lida held bunched in her hand.

"It isn't polite to point," Lucille chided.

"What is it?" he insisted, pointing nonetheless.

Lida held it up, one piece at a time. "It's a swimsuit," she told him. "A bikini."

"Biki . . . " he began, but stopped.

"Bikini," Lida repeated.

"Bikini!" he said, grinning.

"That's very good, Jeff!" Jerry's big voice filled the hall. He was an associate professor in the Geography Department and spoke every word as if it had seismic significance.

"Honey," Lucille whined, "don't encourage him!" She turned the boy around and gave him a little pat to start him off down the hall. "Honestly. And, Lida, I wish you'd . . ." She drew her lips into a little circle, fretting. "I wish you wouldn't answer Jeff's questions. Jerry and I are trying to encourage him to use deductive reasoning."

"Absolutely," Jerry said, winking at Lida over his wife's shoulder.

"Lucille," Lida said, "there is no way your son or anyone

could look at these two pieces of cloth and deduce the word 'bikini.' Believe me, no way."

"Oh, Lida," Lucille said, patting Lida's forearm. "Don't be so serious. I didn't mean to hurt your feelings."

"Now, now, ladies," Jerry said, laying his hand on Lida's shoulder. "I'll tell you what. I'll take Lida for a little walk and tell her all about the way we're raising Jeff, and you take Diana into our bedroom and show her the canopy we made."

He led Lida away, sliding his arm around her, big-brother fashion. "Let her alone," he said, "please?" His arm still hung in place.

"Look. I'm not making a big deal out of this. It's just that. . ." She stopped walking and took a deep breath. "Jer, your wife is an idiot. I'm sorry, but she's a raving idiot."

They walked around the pool and back into the house in silence. When Lucille and Diana met them, Jerry gave Lida a big, friendly squeeze and released her. "She's convinced," he told his wife.

"See?" Lucille said. "That husband of mine can convince anyone of anything."

"He didn't convince me, Lucille, but it sure felt good."

Lucille squealed at the remark as though it had been clever.

Very late that night, Lida's phone jangled.

"Do you know who this is?" a male voice began.

"If I knew," Lida said, "I'd call the police."

"It's Jerry."

"Oh."

"What did you mean when you said that?" he asked.

"Said what?" Oh, God, that Lucille was an idiot.

"That it felt good. You said, 'It sure felt good.' "

"Aw, Jer, I don't know. I guess I meant that it felt good. Just forget it."

"I'm not sure that I want to forget it," he answered.

34

"What do you mean?"

"I mean, I'd like to see you."

"Oh," she said. "Okay, sure."

"When?" he asked.

"I don't know."

"Well, what's a good time for you?"

God, was she *that* desperate?

Afterwards he stood in the bathroom, swabbing his genitals. "I'll get a rash if I don't," he said, turning away.

God, *that* desperate?

She would have called it off. Only, before she could, Jerry was flat on his back in the hospital. He had called her, urging her to visit.

"But your family," she protested, "Lucille."

"She won't be in until eleven."

9

Jackson R.W. Bishop lifted the parcel that had arrived from New York. It was heavier than the others had been. He hoped Duvivier's readers would bear with him through all those bashings and screwings. Would that his own scholarly work be so well received.

He pulled the tab and removed the page proofs. There was a letter as well, already opened, but replaced in its envelope.

"My dear Duvivier," it began.

He looked at the letterhead. Brady State College. In smaller type, Department of English.

He had known for some time that Duvivier had become a kind of cult figure, read by certain sophisticated people as one who offered light escape while, at the same time, not harshly insulting their intelligence. He hoped that the correspondent would be one of these followers, and not the sort who took the brutality, sexual and social, to heart. He knew from experience, however, that academic connections guaranteed nothing. Brady State College.

He thought of the school where he had himself taught. It had been years since he'd conjured its image.

The roads which led to it were not unlike those that led to Pedraza, steep and twisted. Except, of course, the roads to the college had been paved. Thin black ribbons that wound through the lush green New Hampshire hills.

He had conceived the first Duvivier book in New Hampshire. Indeed, it had emerged—like an erection—almost with a will of its own.

At first there were penciled notes on the backs of the mimeographed sheets that came from the departmental office. The notes began to take form at faculty meetings, where, on the first Wednesday of every month, those mimeographed sheets were read aloud.

His scribblings, wherein he either screwed or battered one or several of his students, provided entertainment sufficient to survive the quorum counts, the testy references to *Robert's Rules of Order*, the motions and countermotions.

His colleagues and the various administrators never drew attention to the fact that he wrote through every meeting. They could hardly disapprove. In fact, if the truth be told, they gloried in his eccentricities, for he had brought some measure of fame to their school.

He had published, while yet an assistant professor, a treatise on Renaissance stagecraft. It had been printed with his academic affiliation beneath his name. Many, of course, had churned out articles. This, however, was a book, hardbound and translated into seven languages. When the senior Renaissance man on the staff snubbed him at a party, he knew he would not perish except by his own design.

Later, when that chapter of his life had been brought to its end, he had rubbed salt into the man's wound by bequeathing to the college library the working draft and all revisions of the treatise. And, as a kicker, he had left them a work in progress:

Medieval Pageantry and Its Effect on the Concept of Kingship in the Elizabethan Era.

He leaned back and read Lida's letter, laughing aloud in several spots. Then he searched for paper upon which to write his reply.

10

Jerry was eating breakfast and talking to the man in the opposite bed when Lida came in.

"Hey!" he said when he saw her, stopping mid-sentence and drawing the curtain between the two beds. He pushed the tray away and got back under the sheet.

She began to clear the magazines from the bedside chair.

"No," he said, taking her hand. "Come here." He laid her fingers over his erection. She pulled back, gesturing toward the curtain. "He'll be gone tomorrow," he whispered.

"What about your heart?" He was there for his heart. He was scheduled to have open-heart surgery.

"It's okay, really, come on." He pushed her head down toward his penis, pulling the sheet back. "Please, Lida, it's okay." He had a tube in his leg just below his testicles, and a gauze patch over it which reeked of iodine.

"I'm afraid," she said. "I'm afraid you'll die."

"Please," he repeated, sounding desperate.

He laughed afterward, showing her the little machine strapped to his body. "It monitors my heartbeat," he said. "They're probably going crazy back there."

<p>

He was operated on two days later, then spent five days in intensive care. On the sixth day, he was back in his room.

When she walked in, he was standing in front of the small sink in the room. He had a new roommate now, a bulky black man, and he introduced Lida to him. Then he pulled the curtain that ringed the sink.

He was wearing white support hose and a hospital gown. And Sperry Top-siders. He looked silly.

"You need a garter belt," she told him.

He lifted the gown and pointed his erection at her, laughing. She was mesmerized by the long row of stitches that ran up his thigh and into his groin. "I can walk up the hall now," he said, grabbing a bathrobe.

They stopped by a row of television sets. "I'll show you my heartbeat," he said, pointing at one of the sets. "That one, fourth row down."

"Yours doesn't look like the others."

"That's what you do to me." He laughed, and so did the orderly who was monitoring the sets.

He guided her across the hall. It was a lounge, empty at this hour. They sat on a vinyl sofa and he kissed her. "We," he said, "are going to have a problem with that door."

"What do you mean?"

"It doesn't lock." He began scanning the room, his eyes serious and calculating. He got up and walked over to a table. Someone had been sitting there working on a jigsaw puzzle. He pulled the chair into a corner of the room. "Push that door shut," he directed her.

She did, then went over to the window, yanking on the

40

drapery cord. "This is insane," she said, wondering at her participation. "If I'm ushered from this hospital in disgrace, I'll never forgive you."

He sat on the chair and positioned her over him. "Why aren't you wearing any underwear?" He laughed.

He came almost as soon as he entered her. "Screw you," Lida said. "Next time it's my turn." He got up and wiped his penis against his robe. He started toward the door.

"Oh, please"—she touched his arm—"please, let's stay and talk."

"I'm bushed." He made a tired face. "You really wiped me out." He put his arm around her. "Come on. I've got to get back to bed."

"Talk to me," she demanded.

"I can't talk. I've got to get to bed. You are some kind of tranquilizer." He grabbed her hand and held it, closing his eyes.

"I'll go," she said, disengaging her fingers and wishing he'd object.

"Can you come on Friday?"

She fairly flew into the room and stopped short. There was another man in the bed. "Where is Jerry?" she demanded of the black man to whom she had been introduced.

"He went home yesterday." The man laughed.

Lida began crying and didn't stop until she was home.

Later, Jerry called. "You didn't go to the hospital this morning, did you?"

"Yes," Lida said evenly, "I did."

He gave a half-laugh. "I came home yesterday," he said.

"I discovered that." Her voice was still hard, but the bridge of her nose ached with holding back her tears.

He was silent. Then he said, "I just didn't have a chance to call you until now. I mean, I couldn't call you."

"Where are you?"

"I'm at home."

She strained to hear the sounds behind him. "How is it that you're calling now?"

"They went out," he said. "Well, some of them went out."

She began crying. "Talk to me. I feel so terrible."

He sounded nervous. "I can't really do that right now. You know, little pitchers?"

"Will you call me?" she pleaded.

"Yes."

"Soon?"

"Yes."

She let him hang up. But two weeks later, he still hadn't called.

"Except for the ending," she told Diana, "it makes a rollicking good story." Lida made her voice big, in imitation of Jerry's. "Queen of the Coronary Corridor!"

But Diana was serious. "You really ought to get over this," she said. "He just turned out to be a bastard."

Another bastard. "I know that," Lida said, "but knowing doesn't help. I just feel so fucking stupid."

"Why should you feel stupid? The guy is a jerk. He *deserves* Lucille."

"Nice try, Diana, but *I* behaved like a jerk. I let Jerry Felton turn me into some kind of circus act. And don't you see? The fact that it's Lucille makes it worse?"

42

11

Lida picked up the aerogram in her mailbox and examined its face. Did she know anyone overseas? She turned it over and read the reverse side.

There it was, in lowercase letters: duvivier. She carried it to her desk and opened it with exaggerated care.

As the return address informs you, I live in a very small village in Spain, and letters come to me only most tardily. Accept this, please, in explanation of my late reply.

Your point concerning the childish counterplay (ref: precoital chat; menstrual reference) is well taken. Certainly such bright people as the two involved would not make a point of this. But you must recall that the Duvivier books (I write under three names and to three vastly differing readerships) are popular escapist literature, designed to appeal to millions of people in thirteen languages. As it is, I just manage to get away with the slight chidings and ridicule of conventions that I tuck in amongst the bashings and screwings that make the books popular. My mass reader—the Japanese bank clerk, the French soldier, the American factory worker, the English dock worker—is put off enough by the very mention of menstruation, for he is caught in a convention that heroes never defecate, and women never turn a hero down when he is generous enough to offer the comfort of his bed. These surrenders to the prejudices and preconceptions of the mass must seem to you dull and stupid.

I accept the criticism, but must mention that I use these books only to make money for the two other writers and the rather extravagant and expensive activities in which they engage.

You take a charming little shot at me (and you have a right to, since you were disappointed in your expectations of quality) by assuming that I am in my late 60's and therefore to be forgiven. I am in fact in my early 60's and am *therefore* to be forgiven.

Yours, by the way, was the first letter in English I have received in several months, and I was very pleased to read it.

May I suggest a more romantic and sophisticated look at human love than you will ever get from duvivier (Aren't you, really, tired of his wise-assery?)? Sometime last fall in the United States, Seare and Jolly released a book by Paul Philippe Grisone entitled *Fleur*. I think you might enjoy it.

Thanking you for writing, I am . . .

> Your servant,
> duvivier

Lida wished she had worn a brassiere. She would have tucked the letter in her cleavage. As it was, she opened the collected works of Milton and placed it between *Paradise Lost* and *Paradise Regained*.

She dialed an outside line, then the Library of Congress. "Telephone inquiry, please." While she waited, she wrote his name on the pad. Duvivier. Then, copying him, she wrote it in lowercase letters. She did this across two pages. Then, finally, someone picked up on her call. "Is there any way," she said, tearing the pages free, "I can get the real name of an author using a pseudonym?"

Another wait on hold. Another person.

"Is there any way you can give me the real name," she asked again, "of an author writing under a pseudonym? . . . Yes, that's right."

She drew an eyebrow on the pad, and below it, an eye.

"D as in dog. U. V as in victory. I. V as in victory, yes, again. I, again. E. R. That's right."

She opened Milton and reread the letter, then replaced the book on the shelf. She heard the footsteps of the clerk coming back to the phone. "What's that?" Shit. "Thanks very much," she said, deflated. But wait! He wrote, he'd said, under three different names! "Hey, how about Grisone? Paul Philippe Grisone. G-r-i-s-o-n-e."

"You want the titles or cross-references or what?"

"All that. And, wait a minute . . . " Lida yanked at her middle drawer and produced the list of titles Seare and Jolly had sent. There were eight books on it, and she'd managed to buy all but two. "See if you have something called *Renaissance Stagecraft*."

"This is going to take some time," the clerk said. "And all of this information is available in our card catalog."

"I'm bedridden," Lida told her. "I'd love to come in and do it myself, but I can't."

There was a stiff silence. Then the clerk drew a deep breath. "Hold on," she decided.

She returned with four Grisone titles, though *Fleur*, the book he'd mentioned in his letter, was not among them. The Grisone books were cross-referenced to a Jackson R.W. Bishop, and he, Bishop, had three titles. *Renaissance Stagecraft*? By a Ronald Wendolyn.

I write under three names . . . But now Lida had four: Duvivier, Grisone, Bishop, Wendolyn.

"One more thing . . . " Lida forced a cough.

"Tsk," the clerk replied. But even so, she furnished the dates Lida requested.

❦

The Wendolyn book had been published in the early 1960s. The others, in the '70s. *I write under three names* . . . Ah, Lida decided, but he lived under the fourth. And it was Ronald Wendolyn. It had to be. She wrote it on a separate sheet.

She creased the sheet, making it into a paper airplane. She balanced it on her fingertips. Ronald Wendolyn. It was a fag name. Take him to a party and he'd probably start telling Tallulah Bankhead stories or something.

And if he wasn't a fag, he was probably one of the Wrong Men. Just like all the rest. The Wrong Men, they were legion.

And anyway, maybe the temporary had been wrong. Maybe Ronald Wendolyn had nothing to do with Duvivier and the rest. What did temporaries know?

What was she getting excited about?

The paper airplane bearing the name of Ronald Wendolyn sailed through Lida's office door and landed on the floor in the hall. But not quite on the floor. Actually, it rested atop the abandoned wrappings of a Reese's peanut-butter cup and leaned against an empty milk carton.

Christ, Brady State. There it was in summary. Trash.

Lida knew that she had to get away. To the supermarket, that would be a start.

❦

At the checkout, a woman in front of her, accompanied by a man and a child, presented a personal check.

"Phone number?" the clerk asked.

"Four-three-seven," the woman said, "seven-one-eight-six."

The man shifted to make his impatience known. The child

46

tugged at the woman's hemline, pointing at the candy rack with his free hand.

"Stop it, Bobby!" The woman jerked her skirt free and slapped back at the boy.

The man lowered his fist to Bobby's face and shook it. The child cowered.

"I'll need your driver's license."

The man pulled the wallet from his wife's grasp, jerked a sheaf of cards free, and slammed them on the counter.

Lida, meanwhile, busily examined the Dr. Scholl's display. Here, she thought, is God's plenty.

When she came out of the store, the trio was there again. They were in one of those pickup trucks designed to look like passenger cars. The child pressed his face against the rear window, smearing the pane. The man glared alternately at his wife and at the stockboy hefting bag after bag after bag.

Lida looked back at the truck as she crossed to the lot. It bore a bumper sticker that read "HONK IF YOU'RE HORNY."

"Oh, Ronald Wendolyn," Lida said, squeezing her avocado and sniffing at the brisk fall air, "I feel sick."

She sat on her unmade bed, notebook in hand. It would have to be a light letter, even breezy. He wouldn't want her if he knew how gloomy she'd become. But at the same time, it would have to be sedate. Nothing flirty, nothing sexy. She was through with all that.

He was the perfect out. In his sixties. Probably couldn't get it up anymore. She would be safe.

Still.

She put the pad aside, walked to her dresser, and stood before the mirror. She laid her hands on her hipbones, narrowed her eyes, and mustered a steely objectivity.

Hmmm. She could have a cuter nose, maybe, but basically she was hot shit. She stepped sideways, tossing her head. Her hair lifted, then fell back into place, thick and black and shining. Damn. She could do anything with her hair. And she had those fantastic cheekbones—Jesus, how many times had she heard that? And, oh, those geisha eyes. How long could he resist those geisha eyes? Damn.

She cocked her head and thought and thought.

For starters, she could wear her hair severely. Maybe pile it up the way Diana did.

With her fingers, she raked two luxuriant handfuls to the top of her head. Well, that would *help*.

And if she wore no makeup. Not even a trace.

Of course—she held her arms aloft and backed away from the mirror—there was still the body. Small tits, yes, but that never did seem to matter. She stepped toward the mirror again.

She could play the body down. Slump, maybe. Wear baggy cardigans with pockets stuffed full of Kleenex. Yeah.

And she would—what was that line she'd recently read? Yeah. She would, she resolved, "in her person elevate Plainness almost to a high art."

12

All that he would need for his trip to America was packed in a single leather suitcase. The other things, the household items, his typewriter, and so on, had gone ahead to France.

He walked from room to room, eyeing the shrouded furniture.

The timing had been excellent. He would leave Spain, stop in New York to negotiate the movie rights on the Duvivier series, then take up residence in Pau. Altogether, he would be in the States two, maybe three days. That seemed to him a long time.

He had no faith in coincidence, and thus did not fear discovery. And he'd been back in the States before. He was, by habit, very careful; by nature, very clever. Everything would be all right.

He raised the window and listened for the Land Rover that would carry him to the airport in Madrid. When he heard it, he closed the sash, grabbed his satchel, and walked out into the quiet, cobbled street.

"Señor Beeshop." It was María, his maid. *"Una carta."* She handed him an aerogram, then retreated, her dark clothes merging with the shadows.

He slid the letter into his breast pocket and was off.

He loathed the Madrid terminal. Each year, it seemed, the shops grew tawdrier and the vendors' stands more plentiful. Ah, well, soon Madrid, too, would be part of his past.

His plane was announced and he went to meet it. He carried his suitcase on board. He ignored the sunrise, though it was spectacular: blue-black mountains pressed against a blood-red sky.

The plane lurched out over the ocean as daylight steadily filled the cabin. When it was sufficiently bright, he took the letter from his pocket.

He recognized the name on the flap, but this time she had used her home address. He hoped she would not become a nuisance.

Duvivier was ofttimes very foolish. Paul Philippe, for instance, would never have answered her letter. Paul Philippe would, he suspected, throw this one into the trash, its seal unbroken.

He opened it and began to read. It started off in a typically American way:

> Remember me? A while back I wrote you a huffy little letter about the menstrual number that you did. I found your reply (which was a surprise) wonderfully funny. I'm glad I kept it, because I think I could use your help. I want to disappear, poof, vanish. It occurred to me that I could disappear to Spain, work for you (room, board, a small stipend). I'm a terrific audience, a reasonable critic, an able (though unwilling) typist. I have only been drunk

twice in my life and I'm planning to quit smoking. Despite this letter, I am quite sane. I do menstruate regularly, but I think you can handle it.

Where did she live? He flipped back to the address. Laurel, Maryland. Where was Laurel, Maryland? He had no idea. Why was she writing? What, that is, precipitated her letter? Duvivier could use that sort of information in his next book. A few critics had complained that his women weren't believable.

He pulled a magazine from the pocket of the seat in front of him. He skipped from page to page, impatient. One headline caught his attention—an abominable combination of words: YOUTH WAS SWERVED AS THE FRENCH SWEPT. What could that mean? He read it:

The goings-on in the days leading up to the 25th running of the Washington, D.C., International at Laurel, Md., were bizarre, almost as crazy as the running of the race itself.

He read it again. Yes, that's what it said. Laurel, Maryland, a suburb, apparently, of Washington, D.C. He smiled, replacing the magazine. He would, he resolved, give the novels of Thomas Hardy a second chance.

13

Diana pulled to the side of the road and consulted the map. As far as she could tell, it was over 400 miles from Washington to the New Hampshire border. She was, she deduced, halfway there. Halfway there. A relevant phrase.

Having liberated herself enough to reserve Lida's house for that rendezvous with Lou, she had, when face to face with him, been unable to admit it.

"What would you like to do?" he'd asked.

"Um," she'd said, inadvertently coy.

"I know," he said, "we'll drive to Baltimore. Get a corned-beef sandwich."

And, ramrod of rectitude that she was, or seemed, she'd agreed.

Diana had consoled herself, there in the Pratt Street delicatessen, with balm she'd so often offered Lida. He, Lou, the burly man who sat across from her intently studying the stratified layers of his sandwich, was one of the Wrong Men. He had to be. It was that simple. But she knew now why Lida was never easily consoled.

She thought of Lida, thought of how their situations, hers and Lida's, had reversed. After that awful business with Jerry in the hospital, Lida had withdrawn into celibacy. And she, Diana, was . . . well, ready.

She could hear Lida now, lingering over the details. The long row of stitches. The smell of iodine. The little machine strapped to Jerry's body. Ghastly. And how he'd treated Lida later. Ghastlier still. Poor Lida. "If I were in love with him," Lida had said, "I could take it. But I'm being treated like shit by someone I can't even stand. God, I was doing him a favor! You should have heard him, 'Please. Please.' "

She imagined Lida's list of lovers yellowing, flaking with age. And would she, Diana, compile a list of her own?

Well, she wasn't that ready. Just halfway there.

Diana tilted the rearview mirror and looked at herself: a stranger, albeit a pretty one. Lida had been right. Why, Diana wondered, had she struggled against Lida's every suggestion?

"I'm not talking about a major overhaul," she remembered Lida arguing. "No plastic surgery. No silicone injections." She had been marched to the full-length mirror on the bathroom door. "Look, kiddo," Lida had said, gesturing at Diana's image and delivering the final blow. "I just want you to stop looking as though you're on your way to some bingo."

If Lou hadn't noticed that she had stopped looking that way, *stuff* him! And if Lida hadn't asked if he'd noticed, stuff *her*! Diana pulled back onto the highway, eager to travel the remaining stretch of road.

She suddenly felt free, apart from all restraint. Apart from them all—from Lida, from Lou, from her children. She felt alive! She felt single! And alone, wonderfully alone!

She leaned into the turns, driving faster than she'd ever driven. She passed several signs offering food and gasoline. Finally, when the gas gauge sank perilously low, she followed one of them off the superhighway and onto a two-lane road.

After he had filled her tank and taken her money, the attendant glanced at her out-of-state plate and seemed to scoff. He gave her a mocking stare.

"Is something wrong?" she called, daring him.

He looked away, even reddening a bit.

"Where can I get something to eat?" she asked in triumph.

"What's that?"

"The sign said 'Food.' Is there a restaurant down this road?"

"Yep."

Diana swooped off in search of it.

It was more like a roadside store than a restaurant, despite a weathered sign proclaiming it the latter. There were three cars in the gravel lot parked in no apparent pattern. Diana pulled up beside one of them and cut the engine off.

She wasn't really hungry. The excitement had usurped her need for food. Nonetheless, she had a four-hour drive ahead. She started inside.

Diana regressed. She was instantly embarrassed.

There were shelves bearing grocery items, canned foods, loaves of bread and such, in the foreground. Beyond these was a counter with several stools. Behind the counter, a young girl, seventeen perhaps.

The girl was standing beside a meat slicer which held a huge round of bologna. She stood, semiconscious, pushing it to and fro. Her eyes were closed and her hair hung, limp and dirty, across her forehead. Her skirt was hiked up above one knee, which pressed forward. Her body moved in rhythm to the machine.

Two men sat at opposite ends of the counter. They were watching the girl as though hypnotized by her movement.

Diana stood at the door and steeled herself for retreat.

But the tableau ended. The girl folded the paper over the heap of meat she had accumulated, moistened a sticker to hold it shut, and looking directly at Diana, plopped the package on the counter in front of the man on the left.

He stirred his coffee and nodded, barely noticing. The other man raised a sandwich to his mouth. It would have been harder now to leave than to stay, and so Diana walked ahead and sat on the centermost stool. Woman of the world, ha! Halfway there, indeed!

She took the agenda for the conference from her purse and occupied herself with it. There would be coffee in the library at ten. Then the papers would begin, with hers scheduled to be the third. Then lunch, then more papers. Cocktails and dinner and, she might as well admit it, home.

Still, three years ago, she knew, the quality of the scene she had witnessed would have escaped her. Her mind carried her back further still. She thought of Bill and the pallor of her response to him. Then the sequence moved forward. She thought of her sons, of the kinky black hair that curled in their armpits. Of their voices, deep and deepening.

She would have to call Bill to check on the boys. She heard them already, talking all at once, each accusing the other and demanding that his brother be punished. The hell with it. She would tell them that she couldn't call. Her room had no phone. The switchboard was closed. The lines all over New Hampshire had been severed.

Diana felt good again when she drove on.

Diana was aware that he had been watching her long before she rose to take the podium. She had arranged and rearranged her papers, but always in the same order. He had arrived later than the others, and so they had not been introduced.

"All the while they were talking the new morality . . ." That line from Ezra Pound hammered in her brain.

It was the question-and-answer period she had dreaded, but her fears, she discovered, had been unjustified. She answered their queries easily and well. She half-heard the directions to the room where the luncheon would be served, feeling his eyes, yes, exploring.

And when she arose to go . . .

She snatched up a napkin and an array of silver. He was beside her now.

"You were marvelous," he told her.

But then there was another voice, nearer a rasp. "Hey, Dilworth," it said. "You can't keep this pretty lady all to yourself."

Diana turned and forced a smile.

14

The telephone, it seemed to Lida, always rang when least she needed it. It rang now as she stumbled into the house with a grocery bag that had begun to split. She was out of breath. "Hello," she coughed into the receiver.

"We have never met, my dear," he began.

The bag gave way and cans and oranges rattled across the floor.

" . . . but we have corresponded a time or two. My name is Duvivier."

Lida's heart flashed neon. "God!" she said.

"I am at the Watergate Hotel. Do you think we could have a drink together?"

"Oh, no!" she gasped. "I have to go to traffic court tonight!" Her driving record had finally caught up with her. "Wait a minute! Screw traffic court. When?"

"An hour?"

She looked at the clock. She was wearing jeans and a sweat-shirt. She hadn't shaved her legs, God, since Jerry. Her nail polish was chipped and her hair in need of a shampoo. "Okay," she said, "an hour."

"I'll meet you in the bar," he said.

"Wait a minute. Which bar?" She had never been to the Watergate. She wasn't sure, in fact, that she knew how to get there. And maybe there were several bars. Maybe she'd never find him.

"All right. Go to the check-in desk. You'll see a circular staircase. Follow it to the bottom, and you'll be in the bar."

She sidestepped the mess on the floor and ran upstairs to fill the tub, adding to the litter by discarding her clothes along the way.

She would call Diana. But there was no time. And, damn! Diana was away.

"Jesus!" she shouted, reborn. "Jeeeesus!"

15

"What do you say we skip the afternoon session?" With that, he nudged her. Diana hoped her recoil was not visible.

"It's always the creeps who come right out with it," Lida once advised. "They pretend they're kidding, see? But they're hoping you'll take them up on it."

"Paul Riley," Allen Dilworth muttered in the vicinity of Diana's ear. "He's a neo-Romantic by way of explanation. Swinburne, in fact."

Diana laughed. "I should have supposed it."

Allen handed her a platter, and their fingers brushed and crackled with electricity.

"Oh." Diana laughed. Her face, she felt, was burning.

"Yes," he said, watching her as he had when she read.

The palms of her hands felt soggy. But beyond him she saw Riley, waving them toward two seats that he had saved.

"I think," she wished that she could say aloud, "I've gone stark raving mad."

For amid the banality that Riley's presence imposed upon their talk, she felt aglow—as though, if the room were darkened, she, Diana, could light it.

And Allen? Did he feel that way too? She imagined the overhead lights extinguished, the windows shaded.

But her fantasy was interrupted by her own rote answers to Riley's questions.

"Black school, huh?" Riley put a forkful of food into his mouth and poked Diana again with his elbow. Diana watched him chew, chew, chew. At long last Riley swallowed. "Bet they don't use memos at your school," he said. "Bet they use the drum." He began to beat on the tabletop with his open palms. "Boom-da-da, boom-da-da, boom." The silverware rattled against the china. Riley laughed hard, his face turning a splotchy red.

Allen squirmed uncomfortably. He leaned forward, nearer to Diana, to speak his reprimand. "I say, Paul," he began.

"I know, I know," Riley halted him. "Just making a little joke, that's all. No offense meant."

Allen and Diana sought to break the ensuing silence simultaneously. They both laughed at their clumsy attempt.

"Go on," Allen said.

"No, you go ahead," Diana insisted.

They laughed again, easily. It was as though they'd been laughing together all their lives.

God, had it been this simple all along? The Diana of old would have been demure. No, withdrawn. Would have moved away, afraid that he would see or suspect that she wanted to move toward. In other words, the Diana of old was, as Lida had ended up screaming that makeover day, " . . . a king-sized asshole, that's what! How are they supposed to know what you're afraid of? They think *you're* rejecting *them.* Jesus."

"They *would* reject me," Diana had cried. "They *would* laugh at me. Or just not notice me at all. You don't know. You just don't know."

"God damn it," Lida had said. "Are you going to sit around hankering for the rest of your life? Because nobody is going to rescue you. Nobody is going to know or guess how you feel. Nobody is even going to *care* how you feel. *You* have to make the move. *You* have to make the statement."

"What statement? What are you talking about? I don't know what you're talking about." But Diana did know.

Lida had said it out loud anyway. "You don't have anyone, kiddo, because you look as though you don't want anyone. You look as though you don't and then you act as though you don't."

"I don't want to be laughed at," Diana had said. "My sons will laugh. Men will laugh."

"Bullshit."

"It's so superficial."

"If that's all there is, then it's superficial. But I don't think you have to worry about that."

And now here Diana was, in New Hampshire, with two men flanking her, vying for her favors. Amazing. And all along it had been so simple.

Diana felt bold, as she had earlier on the highway, bold and free. Here, in New Hampshire, she could step out of—or was it into?—character. Here, in New Hampshire, Diana could test, could find out which it was. Out of? Or into?

She leaned back in her chair, the way that Lida often did. She even smiled at Riley. Or rather, she was smiling when she turned his way and even the sight of him chewing did not extinguish the expression on her face.

By the time the name of Allen's predecessor was raised,

Diana was feeling very Lida-like indeed.

"Let's don't get started on him again," Allen cautioned Riley.

"Why?" Diana interrupted. "Is he so disreputable? Does spittle run out of the corners of his mouth? Does he—" She stopped and began to giggle, unable to go quite as far as Lida once had.

Allen laughed uneasily, but laughed nonetheless. But Riley? Riley didn't laugh at all. He sank instead into a pensive silence.

"I'm sorry." Diana sobered, thinking she'd offended him. "Actually I was quoting a friend of mine."

Riley looked at her. "What friend?" he asked.

Diana was perplexed. "I doubt that you know her," she said.

"What friend?" Riley insisted. "What's her name?"

"Her name is Lida," Diana said, instinctively leaning toward the safety of Allen.

"Lida," Riley repeated. "Lida. No. Don't know her."

Had it not been for the arrival of a raspberry mousse toward which all subsequent comment might be aimed, the moment would have routed Diana's newfound confidence. She emitted a number of ooohs and mmmms and yummies before Riley excused himself and lumbered toward the exit. Diana watched him go. She pushed her dish away. "I hate raspberry mousse," she said. "I hate raspberry anything."

Allen grinned at her. "Astonishing," he said.

"Wasn't it? What could have come over him?"

"Oh, Riley?" Allen only now considered him. "I think that your remark—the, uh, one about the spittle—reminded him of someone." He spooned some of the mousse into his mouth. "Mmmm," he said.

Diana found that watching Allen chew was far from disagreeable.

"I've seen this happen once or twice," Allen continued. "Riley apparently had a romance with one of the students.

Long time ago. Whenever anything or anyone calls her to mind, he falls into this—what would you call it? A reverie?"

He paused, but Diana did not answer.

"Actually," Allen told her, spooning up more of the mousse and eyeing the serving that Diana had shoved aside, "if you'll come home with me later, I'll give you the full story. It's our campus whodunit. And how's this for a hook?" He dabbed at his lips with his napkin, delaying the line. "The student? Christine Rivers?"

Diana nodded.

"She's dead." His eyes glinted with glee. "Murdered."

Diana dropped her eyes, toyed with the hem of the table-cloth. *If you'll come home with me later,* he had said. *If you'll come home with me!* She felt his hand on her shoulder.

"Have I gone too far?" he asked. "Are you shocked and dismayed?"

Diana didn't look up. "Only shocked," she said.

"Ah. Then you'll come?"

Diana sat, gathering courage. At least twice, she thought. She looked up now, looked at him steadily. "I'll come," Diana said.

They sat together while the recitations droned on. Diana basked in Allen's presence until the readings were over. And then, she was suddenly afraid to stand lest her skirt be stained. Worse, she sensed that he knew why she hesitated, towering beside her, offering his hand.

It was an odd little house with Tudor affectations. It lay flush against the side of the hill. From the window of the bedroom upstairs, Diana had a striking sense of height.

In the spring, he told her, daffodils would blanket the steep slope. In the summer, the leaves of the trees would obscure the stream that sparkled at the base of the hill.

They stood at the window a long time, Diana with a fullness in her lips and her breasts, a crazy knowledge that inside her body, cells and molecules were straining toward him.

Poor Lida? No. Lucky Lida. To have done this a thousand times.

His lips teased across her forehead and his fingertips slipped inside the collar of her blouse and along the base of her neck. He undid the clasp of the pearls that she always wore.

It had an underwater quality, a weightlessness, slow and buoyant. Though she could not remember taking it down, her hair hung in tangles past her shoulders.

His tongue slid like satin along her legs, his mouth like velvet, opening, closing.

Just before she fell asleep, she heard him say, with genuine amazement, "Jane Austen?"

16

Lida hesitated, her eyes falling on each man in the room. There were several. She concentrated on the ones past sixty.

At a table in the back, a man stood and beckoned to her. Too young. She turned away, continuing her search. No one, however, seemed to be waiting for her.

The man did not resume his seat, but walked toward her. She measured him: pale blue spectacles, Mick Jagger mouth, the tensile movement of a street fighter, knife in hand. Nice, she thought, but not the reason I'm here.

Then he said her name.

"Why is it I thought you were older?" She eased into a chair.

On the table were several packs of matches, one, she noted, from a supper club that often made the Washington gossip columns. There was, as well, a heap of bills in varying denominations.

He didn't reply to her question, but sat regarding her.

Lida felt very country-mouse.

65

17

Ronald Wendolyn had built the house largely on the proceeds of his book, a heftier sum than he had believed a scholarly work could earn. His reputation, though augmented by that volume, had been constructed much earlier.

The first stone, as it were, was laid in the presence of the committee that had been elected to recruit him.

He remembered the event, the table around which they hovered, these stereotypes of the academic world. He had taken them aback by his attire: sport slacks, a turtleneck sweater, a small silver medallion dangling from a chain. He had deliberated at length about what, in 1961, would sufficiently affront their studied informality, their button-down lives and suede-patch intellects.

His credentials allowed him such extravagances. He had, not the customary single doctorate earned in a long span of poverty, but two—one in English literature, another in theater—plucked from the grove in rapid succession. Ronald Wendolyn was twenty-nine years old.

"Dr. Wendolyn"—the chairman gestured at a vacant chair—"do sit down."

No one had risen when he entered the room. He met each man's eyes before descending to them. "*Mr.* Wendolyn, if you don't mind. If I were to insist that everyone use my proper title"—he gave them a slow smile—"it would get rather silly, don't you think?"

This statement was met with artificial laughter.

The thrust and parry began, child's play. They were waiting, he knew, to revenge themselves upon him. That was all right. He thrived on their envy.

Then it came.

"Tell me, Wendolyn . . . " The interviewer leaned back in his chair, the tone of his voice serving as a nudge to his cronies. "Does anyone in theater have any balls?"

Wendolyn could not believe it. So meager, this attack. He had hoped for something more devious, more intelligent. Pity. "Is everyone here"—he stood, spread his hands on the surface of the table, and asked, his pronunciation polite and impeccable—"an asshole?"

And then he left.

In the days that followed, of course, they had made him a grand offer. He wired a negative reply. Then another came, grander still. This, he accepted.

And so, his days on the small New Hampshire campus began.

His students, he discovered, recorded his witticisms in their notebooks with unyielding solemnity. Indeed, mangled versions of his best lines were returned on examinations at the end of each semester. His colleagues were little better, their comprehension, when it came, tinged with discomfort.

An occasional scatological remark, when it was necessary or when it was fun, gave him a thin link to status as a "regular guy," but even in those instances, many felt that he went too far. While the word "prick" had become quite common, for example, the use of "cunt" and "fuck" had not, even in the locker-room atmosphere of departmental meetings. It amused Wendolyn to broaden the scope of his colleagues' idle chatter and, at the same time, dazzle them with his ability to subtly leaven the cultivated with the coarse. This he did by judicious timing, practiced inflection, and a delivery that enabled him to say the words evenly, with no here-comes-the-naughty drop or see-if-I-can't lift of volume.

It was natural that campus speculation, then, focused in the main on Wendolyn's sex life.

Though most men declared him to be homosexual, none could offer even the slightest proof. And Wendolyn was defended against these accusations by, of all people, the faculty wives—those with widely advertised assets as well as the ones who denied them with good tweeds and support stockings.

Ronald Wendolyn was innately attractive to these women, and often they permitted their husbands to tup them, conjuring all the while his wiry image: lips drawn back with lingering ease, eyes intent and cold. No, they assured their husbands, no one as sexy as Wendolyn could be queer.

It was Paul Riley, the man who had badgered Wendolyn at that first committee meeting, who hit upon it. "Hell," he said to his friends as they drove past the newly acquired Wendolyn property. "He's probably up there right now, jerking off."

Actually, it was not so simple. His masturbatory ritual, in those early days, had been quite elaborate. Even then, however, he had managed to edit the process, as it were. By the time he reached New Hampshire, for instance, he no longer required the candles. The Gregorian chant, while it enhanced his pleasure, could be dispensed with when the situation so suggested—in hotel rooms and such.

But sexual release was never an end, only the means by which he gained the concentration that his work required.

Such was not the case, apparently, with the rest of the faculty and with certain of the students. Indeed, he often felt like a child standing for a stolen moment on the landing of a great staircase, watching the dance in the ballroom below. A minuet: patterned procession of couples, of exchanges, of whisperings between those exchanges.

He derived his satisfaction from the manuscript which lay on the table before him. It had not yet evolved into the series that would carry Duvivier to fame. It had, however, gone beyond the exercise that was its beginning.

He had started by creating dialogue between extraordinary people, the sort he would never find here, nor anywhere. The words would fall to the page without effort. Then he would find features to fit the speakers, then names, and later, settings.

He would rush home after office hours had ended and sift through the cardboard box, rereading the pages greedily and often. Once every week or so he would stack the sheets and measure their bulk between his fingers. Rather, he thought, like a puppetmaster stroking his dolls in the backstage darkness.

He knew that his writing was good, and feared only that it was too good. Not childish, not foolish enough for this world.

He decided to add sex and, for good measure, savagery, to his text. Object lessons in both, separate or in concert, abounded.

Yes, that would sew it up.

He looked forward to the Thanksgiving recess and the time that it would bestow. But there was, suddenly, more time still.

He had heard it on the radio in the smoker. The music was interrupted and an announcer cleared his throat. "We interrupt this program to bring you a special news bulletin. The President of the United States has been shot. President John F. Kennedy has been shot and has been taken to Parkland

Memorial Hospital in Dallas, Texas." An awkward pause, and the music resumed.

Wendolyn looked around the room, but no one else was there. He picked up his jacket and was about to zip it closed when the music broke again. The President of the United States, the voice said, was dead.

The door burst open. It was Paul Riley, blithering."Did you hear?" he asked. When Wendolyn nodded, Riley left the room.

Wendolyn began to walk, not on the concrete paths that crisscrossed the grounds, but on the grass, green gone brown. He watched the news spread in predictable pantomime. Girls clapped their hands over their mouths, or covered their eyes, or fumbled for hankies. Men stared at the ground, or shivered, or cursed. One dared to shrug, and the girl he was with slapped him. "Hey," the boy called after her, "come back here!"

Wendolyn viewed all this with interest, but no involvement. It meant nothing to him, though he knew better than to admit it. When classes were canceled for the remaining few days before the official recess, he, aping the rest, slumped sadly and retreated to his home.

And his manuscript.

✿

She came the following day.

"Can I come in?" she asked when he opened the door. It had just begun to snow and the flurries stuck to her hair and even her eyelashes.

He did not answer, but opened the door to admit her. Christine Rivers. Why had she come?

She misread the look on his face. "Don't worry," she said, "no one will miss me. They're all glued to their teevee sets."

Why was she here?

"The Kennedy thing," she explained, "it's got them all

70

hypnotized. There isn't anyone out anywhere. They're all watching it on television, over and over, the car, the Secret Service men, the doctors at the hospital." She handed him her coat and he took it, laid it over his arm. "Hey," she said, "you *do* know about the Kennedy thing, don't you?"

He shook his head yes. Why was she here?

"And the killer. They've already got the killer."

"Why are you here?" he asked.

She leaned down, undid the laces of her shoes, and slid them off. The snowflakes in her hair had turned to little glass beads. "Nothing good on television," she said. "If I went to a movie—assuming there would be a movie open—no one would ever speak to me again. So I decided to act out my fantasies." She walked past him into his study.

He followed her. "Your fantasies?"

"Sure. All last year I used to daydream about sleeping with you. I thought it was time I did."

He smiled at her bravado. "I'm sorry," he said, "but I'm working."

"Go ahead, finish. I'll amuse myself." She wandered off to inspect the other rooms.

He took the coat to the hall closet and placed it on a hanger.

She was in the living room, noisily tending the fire. He glanced down at her shoes. They were wet. That meant she had walked, and it was at least three miles.

He went to his desk, slid the manuscript to safety, and returned with several sheets of bond. He wadded them, stuffed them inside the shoes, and carried the shoes to the room where she waited.

She was draping her knee socks from the mantel. "Just like Christmas, isn't it?" she said. Her hair had begun to frizz as it dried. The firelight played along its edges.

He stooped to set the shoes on the tiles. "I'll drive you home," he offered.

"Eventually."

"When you're dry." He stood and turned toward her.

71

She laughed. "I'm never dry." She fell back into a chair and raised her skirt. Her bare legs picked up the light.

"That isn't a very subtle pose." He wondered at the calm of his voice.

"Subtlety is a waste of time," she told him. But she pulled the skirt a bit lower. "It's a nice fire," she said, "but it's still cold in here."

"You're too accustomed to the overheated rooms in Ward Hall."

"Hmmm. So you know where I live." She sounded very smug.

But he was startled. He thought of Ward, an ugly red-brick square with pipes that clanked and groaned each time the steam rushed through them. He had heard their resonant struggle many times as he walked past the building. The girls kept their windows open all year long. Had he seen her at one of those windows? Was that how he'd known? Perhaps she'd mentioned it last term, in class.

She seemed to know that he was thinking of the course—the honors offering, where they'd examined eighteenth-century adaptations of Shakespearean plays. "You *have* forgiven me for that paper, haven't you?"

He laughed. "Forgiven you? It was the high point of my tenure here." She had vigorously defended Colley Cibber's emendations, claiming that Cibber's sense of theater far exceeded Shakespeare's. Defiance, even among the honors students, had not yet become fashionable. He had been amused, not merely by the challenge she had raised, but by the answers the others in the seminar had mustered: his own introductory lectures rephrased, and very badly at that. "Your classmates, my dear, are flaming assholes, every one."

"I'm glad you remembered," she said.

18

"Yes," Allen said, agreeing with Diana, "it *is* a wonderful house." He paused to listen, then rose from the table to pull the tea kettle from the burner before it could whistle. "And, as I suggested earlier, a house with a history."

"Oh, yes, the promised history." From behind, Diana noted the hair that bristled on his calves, the plaid of his bathrobe beginning at the crease of his knees.

He poured the steaming water into the teapot. The faint scent of orange filled the room. "Yes. This is Wendolyn House. Named after the fellow who once lived here. He either built this house or had it built. I'm not sure."

"Is he famous?"

"Infamous."

He turned and carried the pot to the table, watching Diana's face. "Perhaps the story should wait," he said.

"No, go on," Diana assured him.

19

"What would you like to drink?" he asked.

"A vodka gimlet," Lida said. That was probably a stupid drink.

"On the rocks? Straight up? How?"

"On the rocks." She was convinced that she had just compounded her blunder. When the drink came, she downed it like lemonade.

The waitress appeared again.

"Another?" he asked.

"Yes."

"Wait," he told the girl. "We'll buy a round for those young ladies over there." He gestured past Lida to another table.

Lida swiveled. File clerks, she thought.

"Does that make you uncomfortable?"

"No." It did.

"Shall we ask them to join us?"

"Join us! No!"

He laughed at her.

"Why would you want them to join us?" She saw him lying naked on an oriental throw, bare-bosomed women ministering. "I really want to know."

"It's nothing. I just wondered how you'd react to the suggestion."

"How did I?"

"With outrage."

Edith Bunker playing opposite James Mason. Oh, shit.

20

Wendolyn felt his penis stir, like a divining rod. It lifted against his trousers, huge and insistent. He listened, expecting to hear the fabric tear and see his cock, live and pink and terrible, levitating in the half-light.

The image made him laugh. He converted the laughter to what he thought was his advantage. "I think, really," he said offhandedly, "that I should take you home."

"You're afraid of me, aren't you?" Christine Rivers sat up, balancing on the edge of the cushion as if about to spring. "I know. You're afraid you won't be able to get it up." Her eyes met his, but her hand jutted forward to discover the error of her surmise. She spread her fingers over the bulge in his pants, her smile widening. "Let's go upstairs," she said.

He must have followed her. "I'm going to undress," he said casually, "and I'd suggest you do likewise."

But she didn't. She propped both pillows against the head-board and leaned back, as if to read. She watched him fumble with the buttons at his wrist.

He looked down at her, noting the absence of color in the gray-lit room. Her hair, bold black against the stark pillow, her mouth gray against the lighter gray of her face. Her skirt gone black, her sweater drained white.

"Aren't you going to undress?" he asked gently, wondering if he should kiss her, touch her, reach to unclasp the waistband of her skirt. He sat beside her to remove his shoes and socks.

"I don't want to undress," she said. "I'll freeze to death." She braced her feet against the mattress, raising her ass. "But, look . . ." She slid her panties off and tossed them to the floor. "We can still do this."

He let his trousers down. When she spread her legs, he knelt between them and closed his eyes.

The walls of her vagina were slick. They exerted a plump pressure which, he was forced to admit, was superior to that of his hand. He wondered how he might duplicate that quality when alone again. Perhaps by using both hands, warming them, wetting them.

But her movement subtracted from his pleasure. He had hoped to maintain the rhythm he had practiced over long years of solitude, but could not. She rolled and bobbed and writhed, opposing him, it seemed. Like dancing with an inept partner.

Not only that. She made sounds. He recognized them as those he had seen on the pages of the books he had been examining of late. Words drawn into streams of type or elongated by hyphens. The orthography of the authors, he decided, had been accurate.

But all of this interrupted his imaginings and thus held his orgasm at bay. And, after the first half hour Ronald Wendolyn wanted very much to come.

The trick was to stop thinking. Then he would come. If she would stop moving and he would stop thinking about how much he wanted her to stop moving, he would come.

But she *had* stopped moving. Her vagina was constricted and dry. And she was silent now. He ground and pumped and ground and pumped and still he could not come.

It was probably her clothes, woolens that scratched at his stomach and his thighs. He ached from the rubbing and thought that blisters would raise where he had, for so long, been scraping against the fabric.

He heard himself grunt, then gasp, and gasp again. Sweat rolled into his eyes and burned. He was unable to end it, this struggle, and hated that Christine Rivers had witnessed it. Her invasion of his privacy was so total now.

He was grateful for the darkness that had swallowed the room, glad he did not have to see her face. Was she weary? Was she in pain? Worst of all, was she bored? He imagined her expression, the cynical twist of her upper lip, the deliberate glaze of her eyes. Then he heard her. She wanted him to hear.

Christine Rivers lay in Ronald Wendolyn's newly violated bed and counted the strokes. Counted, out loud, the number of times he had poked his virgin organ inside her. She was on stroke 757, and now, in severe monotone, she told him it was 758, then 759.

"Seven hundred and six—"

Ronald Wendolyn rested all of his weight on his right forearm, drew his left hand back, and let it fly, full-force, at the spot where her voice had arisen.

Had there been any trace of lubricant, he would have been thrown from her body. But there was none. Their bond held despite the impact of the blow.

At once she became a vigorous participant again, pushing up at him with little fists and raising her hips high off the bed. And she made, all the while, a deep, gargling sound. One he hadn't read of. He pushed her wrists back against the mattress and pumped until she stopped gargling, stopped moving. Still, he hadn't come.

He withdrew angrily, painfully. His erection mocked him and his testicles felt like sinkers. He stood, took a cigarette from the night table, and groped for matches.

She said nothing.

He struck the match and, with a rush of courage, looked down at her. And then he came, doubling over with the thrust of it, splashing semen on his legs and his stomach and on the carpet. The cigarette fell from his mouth unlit.

He recovered and switched the bedside lamp on. He gaped at her and she gaped as well, but at some distant thing. Blood bubbled at her mouth and rolled in gooey streams from her nose, which was swollen, distorted. Her sweater was stained maroon, with little spatters here and there. Her hair was lank.

He tried to lift her, and was startled. Not by her weight—he had read enough to expect that—but by a cramp in his hand. He yanked it away reflexively, and she fell back onto the bed.

He turned the light off and stood at the window regarding the snow. What would he do?

He went downstairs and put a sheet of bond into the type-writer.

He would gather her belongings, remembering the knee socks first. They would be dry now. He would take them from the mantel, lovingly.

Then he would remove the paper from inside the shoes and toss the little wads on the embers. Then roll the socks and place them inside one of the shoes.

Now her panties. He would go upstairs, treading softly, though there was no need to do so, and bring her panties down.

It would be laborious, what with the pain in his hand twanging, twanging. But he would wad the panties and place them inside the other shoe.

And now the body. He would drag—or perhaps carry—her body to the car.

He would prop it carefully in the passenger seat. It would lean against the door.

He would drive slowly, because of the snow. The snow would swirl, filling the beams of his headlights. The wiper blades would barely clear the space on the windshield before the spot would fill again.

Where would he take her? And would he say *her* or *it*?

Ah! He would take her to that billboard on the edge of town, backing into the glare of lights that surrounded the sign.

He would open the car door and tug at her sweater. But wait! If she were leaning against the door . . .

He would open the door and she would fall from the car, onto her face. He would pull her, with much exertion, behind the lattice that formed the base of the sign. And now he would return to the car, fetching her shoes and her coat. God, her coat. He had almost forgotten.

He wondered, would there be blood where she had fallen? No. He would see an indentation, that was all. An indentation already filling with snow.

And the tracks his tires had made? They, too, would be hidden almost at once.

No cars would come, of course, and no pedestrians. He would be safe. So safe that he would dare to scrape the snow from the back window before driving on.

He would look, just once, in the rearview mirror. Inject some humor here. In the rearview mirror he would see the billboard. The one that showed a service-station attendant, close up, grinning at a little red can of Winn's Friction Proofing. He, the callow murderer, would laugh all the way home.

21

"Shall we go to dinner?" he asked Lida.

"I'm not sure I can walk," she said.

"I'll help you." He led her toward the dining room.

The waiter presented him with a thick black binder. The wine list. "You choose," he said, handing it across to her.

"I don't know anything about wine," she told him, flipping through the plastic-covered pages and pondering the selection. When she saw the waiter approaching again, she pointed to a very plain label and said, "This one." She had studiously avoided reading the prices that were typed at the bottom of each page. She hoped it was neither terribly cheap nor terribly expensive.

❦

The bottle arrived and was uncorked. The waiter aimed at Duvivier's glass, but he covered it with his hand. "It was the lady," he said, "who ordered the wine."

The waiter scowled, then poured a bit into Lida's glass.

"Oh, God," she said, "does this mean I have to sniff it and gargle it and slosh it around in my mouth?"

"No"—he laughed—"only American businessmen do that. All you have to do is look at it and nod."

Lida nodded.

❦

She managed dinner.

"What can I do, where can I take you, what can I buy you," he asked, pushing the asparagus he had ordered from one side of his plate to another, "in order to make this evening one that you'll remember?"

"How about dessert?" Lida said.

22

Wendolyn slouched at his typewriter and read again what he had done. He saw that it was good. But could he, with the same godlike stroke, revive her?

He imagined the sort of entrance she would make. She would be hesitant, seeing him there. Yes, brash as she was, she would still be hesitant.

He typed some more, describing the girl's descent into the room where he sat, his back to the doorway.

She would stand, breathing heavily, wiping her damp palms against her skirt. She would visibly gather herself, regain a semblance of her earlier bravado.

But what would the dialogue be like? She had been injured, after all. What would Christine Rivers, in a circumstance like this one, say?

"Jesus Christ," she would whine behind him. "I think you broke my nose."

Wendolyn typed on.

"Hey, what the hell is this? You break my nose and then you come down here and type?" Whimpering her way across the room into the circle of light. "I feel dizzy," she would say, leaning against the desk.

His fingers fell heavily upon the keyboard, jamming several letters. He stood. "I'll get you to a doctor," he would say. "I'll take you to the infirmary. I'll get some ice." Her noisy weeping. He could hear her energetic wails, even when he ran the tap over the ice tray. He would fold a towel around several cubes of ice and return with the compress.

"What do I look like?" Petulant now, tossing the towel aside as though it were a pillow. "Get me a mirror."

"Does it hurt?"

"No. It feels . . . I don't know, big. It just feels big."

He went upstairs, returned with his hand mirror and her panties.

She would look at herself, propping the mirror against his typewriter. "Oh, Christ," she said. Her lip trembling when she touched her nose. Her hands shaking too, briefly. "I thought you'd be different," she said, tossing her head back and covering her face again with the towel.

The desk would be wet where the towel had rested. "I'll get a plastic bag," he would say.

"Why?" Panic edged her question.

"Relax. I'm not going to suffocate you. The ice is melting, that's all."

"Oh," she said.

He went off again, grateful for this minor respite.

"I really thought you'd be different," she called. "I really thought so."

"I'm sorry," he shouted back. He emptied half a loaf of bread onto the counter and returned with the empty wrapper. He handed it to her.

"I don't mean about being a lousy fuck," she said, pushing the towel inside it. "Most of the men around here are. I mean about hitting me." She grew introspective. "He hits me," she said, more to herself than to him. "God, does he hit me. But never in the face. Never once in the face. But the son of a bitch hits his wife, too. He told me."

"I think I'd better take you to the infirmary," he said. "It's after seven and they close at eight."

"After seven! Oh, no! I'm supposed to meet someone!" She handed him the plastic pouch. "I'll tell you what. You let me off at that billboard. You know, the one on the edge of town?" She wiggled into her panties. "I'll be all right."

Gentle reader, thought Wendolyn, do I wake or sleep?

23

"I'm really sorry I brought this Wendolyn business up. It doesn't fit in with . . . " Allen looked at Diana, wondering which word to choose. An easy word. "With this," he said, putting his hand atop hers.

"Monster!" Diana tossed her napkin at him. "You've got my curiosity aroused."

"Only that?" he said in mock dismay. Then he grew serious. "None of it matters anyway," he said. "As Riley has so often reminded me, it was long before I came. None of my business, really. And Wendolyn is dead. If he weren't dead, I wouldn't be here."

"What are you talking about? Did you replace him on the staff? Are you equally infamous? What on earth is all this about?"

"I see before me"—he raised his hand to his brow in the standard communing-with-the-spirits pose—"a reader of

John Dickson Carr, of Michael Innes. Maybe even," he lowered his voice, playing sinister, "Duvivier."

"Tell me, Allen," she persisted. "Leave out the gory parts if you have to, but tell me."

"Ah, if I leave those out," he said, "there will be no story to tell." Then he pursed his lips, grew pensive. "Perhaps there isn't much of one as it is. It's been hard to piece it together, since everyone who had a hand in it—except for Riley, of course—has moved on."

"How did Riley have a hand in it, whatever *it* is?"

"He knew the victim. And he knew the murderer as well."

"The victim," Diana said. "Christine Rivers!"

"Yes."

"And the murderer!" She gestured around the room. "What's-his-name!"

"Ronald Wendolyn. Yes. I'm frankly surprised, from what I've learned, that no one did *him* in. Rumor has it he was roundly hated, a man that no one could stand. Lord knows, Riley goes purple at the mention of his name. Even now."

"Well"—Diana was matter-of-fact—"if Wendolyn murdered Riley's girlfriend, I can see that he might."

Allen looked up abruptly. "Ah, but Riley doesn't know. Only *I* know. The murder, officially, was unsolved."

"But . . ."

"Wendolyn was never a suspect. He stayed on here in perfect safety for some years. And then he died—an auto accident."

"But . . ."

"He left some evidence behind, here, in Wendolyn House. That, too, went undiscovered. Until I came along."

"And the police never revealed it?"

"Police? I never told them. I've told no one. Except you"—he laughed—"just now."

"But why not?"

He looked at Diana, considering. "I suppose I should be honest?"

She nodded yes. "Of course."

"I . . ." He was wary.

"Tell me," Diana said.

Allen sat as though taking the witness box. "As academic slots go," he began, "this one is a plum. Lots of money. And, of course, this house. Ronald Wendolyn, you see, left quite a bundle behind. All of that money—and the money that comes in still—goes to endow the renowned Wendolyn professorship."

"And if Wendolyn were exposed as a murderer . . ."

"Quite so. The position, with all of its attendant pomp and privilege, would be abolished."

Diana stared at the floor. "But didn't anyone else ever suspect?"

"No one. Not until I came across the evidence one day, here, when I was dusting the mantel. That mantel in there. Think of it! *Dusting off the mantel!* Like a detective story. Until then, no dark deed was ever pinned on him. There aren't even rumors, except for the rumor that no one could stand the man."

"Well, if no one suspected him of killing Christine Rivers, why did everyone hate him?"

"I think he was just arrogant. I heard that, after that Renaissance stagecraft thing was published, he went around saying he'd tossed it off in a couple weekends. It drove the drones crazy, of course. Half of the people around here closet themselves away with what they call their 'life's work.' You know, the classic academics."

"You don't mean *you* aren't doing *your* life's work?"

"Ah, but I *am*." He feigned offense. "Mine is the seduction of Jane Austen scholars. Lady scholars, of course. Nothing queer about me."

"And was Ronald Wendolyn queer?"

"Worse than that! I don't know if I can bring myself to tell you."

"Tell me." Diana moved toward him, affecting menace.

"Well, at faculty meetings, Wendolyn is said to have . . .

89

No, I can't tell you."

"I know," Diana said, "he snored."

"Worse."

"He whispered!"

"Far worse." He put his arms around her.

"I know," she said, rubbing her forehead against the stubble on his chin. But then she forgot whatever it was she'd meant to say.

An ease was rising around them, the way dough rises: steadily, immensely. An ease that was domesticity, the sort that Lida would—Diana thought fleetingly—have jangled in upon with an offhand "Isn't this cozy?" It was what Diana gave, and, therefore, what she got.

24

They were in the elevator now. Lida hadn't even noticed which button he had pressed. She followed him down the long corridor and into his room. "I've had too much to drink," she said, "and too much to eat. I really just want to relax."

"Yes," he agreed, "it would be very nice to relax."

How was Lida to know that he meant it? That it was relief which his voice expressed, and not exasperation. Shit. She felt clumsy, stupid—all wrong, somehow. What could she say to impress him, catch him off base, and fast?

"Hey . . ." She snatched at his arm. "I almost forgot to tell you. I know your real name!"

He turned a light on and looked at her, recalling their correspondence. He had given her Grisone. How had she learned Bishop? "Very good," he said. "What is it?"

Lida crossed her fingers and hoped. It all rested with that Seare and Jolly temporary. "It's Wendolyn," she said.

"Ronald Wendolyn." She felt his muscles tighten under her grasp. She had scored. "Surprised you"—she laughed—"didn't I?"

"Where did you get that name?" he asked gently.

"The Library of Congress." It was only half a lie. Or half the truth. But the whole truth was so convoluted. So I-said and she-said. She would lose his attention. Or make him think she'd flushed him out like some fanatic.

"Well . . ." He reached for his cigarettes, forgetting to offer her one. His hand quaked, but very slightly. "I'm delighted to know that even the illustrious Library of Congress doesn't know my real name." He produced a short, derisive laugh.

"That isn't it?" Lida took the pack from his hand and pulled a cigarette for herself. Damn that silly girl!

But he said, "No. That's merely one of the names I've used. One of my authors."

She brightened. "It's Bishop, then."

He smiled and shook his head no.

"You said you write under three names," Lida taunted, "and I know four. Duvivier. Grisone. Bishop. And Wendolyn. One of them has to be real."

He didn't answer.

"What *is* your real name, then?"

"I won't tell you." He made it seem a joke.

"I'll find out," Lida said, dropping the cigarettes onto a dresser and walking toward the bathroom.

"Wait a minute." He was wondering how far she would take the search and how he might stop her. It had been a mistake to label Wendolyn one of the authors. She might find that silly book. One of the early copies, one with his photograph, the name of the school. He improvised a way of checking. "Did you read the Grisone book I suggested? *Fleur?*"

"No. You're not going to like this, but I wasn't able to get it. I couldn't find it in any library, and no bookstore would order a single copy. I finally gave up."

"Well"—he sat with her on the edge of the bed—"let us devise a very clever way for you to get hold of that book." At least he could find out the effect of the wine and of the drinks she'd had. "Um," he thought aloud.

"Can't you just send it to me?"

"That wouldn't be any fun. No. What I'd like you to do is call Carol Bradley at Seare and Jolly. She is Jolly's mistress."

Lida laughed. "Carol Bradley," she repeated.

"Tell her that you had a drink with someone who, oh, drank dry vermouth with a twist of lemon.Then say that you would like a copy of the book. Can you remember that?"

"Vermouth, twist of lemon." Yeah, he had been drinking that in the bar. "Sure. And then what?"

"Then nothing. She'll send you a copy." Was that complicated enough? He thought not. But from it he could deduce the extent of her interest in him. But wait. Perhaps it had been worse to introduce this air of intrigue. Perhaps that, in itself, would spur her on. But no. Even without the intrigue, tonight would spur her on. After tonight, surely, she would read all of his books, even the Wendolyn. Duvivier had been a fool to call her. But maybe the mistake could be rectified. If he handled it well. "Go on to the bathroom," he said.

She went into the bathroom and closed the door behind her. He pushed it open. "I have to . . ." she began.

"I know," he said, "you have to pee. Well, go ahead. Pee."

She started to push the door shut again, but he was stronger than she. "I hate this Take Seven mentality that Americans have. I really hate it. Forget about Take Seven, please, because in Takes One through Six, people pee. They also belch. And they wake up very smelly in the morning. And don't laugh, because I'm very, very serious." He was ranting.

Lida sat on the toilet with her underwear around her knees. He still stood in the open doorway. "I can't," she said.

"All right." He slammed the door and yelled from behind it, "All right. You're American, through and through. Repressed. Oppressed. Et cetera."

"If you keep this up," she hollered back, "I'll never be able to."

"How do they do this to people? How have they managed to produce a whole race incapable of performing the simplest bodily functions in the presence of each other?"

"If it's any comfort to you," she screamed back, "I usually run the water so that people can't *hear* me pee." That wasn't true, of course. "So shut up and listen."

She came out buttoning herself.

"I was sure that you'd undress in there as well," he said. He laid a single finger on her chin. Something about her. What was it about her? "I'm not being very nice to you, am I? But I'm just teasing." He smiled, reached for her hand, and kissed it. She knew, she knew. "The first time you had sex with a man, what was it like?"

"You're crazy." She laughed at him.

"I want to know."

"It was awful. I really didn't want to. I did it so that he'd want me. And when it was over, I felt awful."

"Have you ever had sex with a woman?"

"Why are you asking me these things?"She pulled away from him.

"Have you?"

"No." She stepped out of her shoes and sat on the bed. "You're scaring me," she said.

"Have you ever made love with an animal?" he asked her.

"You're trying to scare me away, aren't you?" She un-clasped her necklace and laid it on the night table. "Sure. Six gazelles and a pig."

He hoped he would not have to kill her.

94

25

These were the free days Wendolyn had hoped for, and yet he did not fill them as he'd planned. His typewriter stood uncovered, sheets of bond scattered beside and atop it. Sheets upon which he had lately written. Sheets he had no desire to read.

Oh, he tried to work. But when he approached his typewriter, or indeed, his desk, he felt faintly dizzy. Like a Victorian maiden in a swoon. So he chided himself. But the self-deprecation did not break the heady spell.

What disease could he have? Hypoglycemia? Cancer? Flu? Perhaps some debilitating gas was seeping into parts of his house? Yes. Near his desk. And upstairs.

For when he went to his bedroom, he was overcome by the same faintness. This was accompanied by a cloying odor which awakened him whenever sleep did come. He sniffed at his pillow in the darkness.

And thought, inexplicably, of a former student. Christine something. Christine . . . Christine Rivers.

It seemed he had dreampt of her. She'd made an appearance on his doorstep, diamonds in her hair, and then she'd come inside. And then . . . his mental screen went blank and the dizziness came again. He strained to remember the dream. Diamonds. No, rubies. Blood-red rubies spilling from her hair onto her face. His penis lifted, as if pleased with the memory. But he felt fainter than he'd ever felt, and beads of sweat burned cold on his forehead.

Malaria. Tuberculosis.

He wiped his brow and considered the way his fingers ached. He added this symptom to the dizziness. What might it be? Tetanus. Polio. And was it somehow related to the pages that cluttered his once-tidy desk downstairs? Was it somehow related to his inability to work?

Dementia praecox. Hell, the vapors.

For the first time in his life, Ronald Wendolyn was glad when classes resumed at the college.

"Is your name Riley?"

"No," Wendolyn said, eyeing with distaste the vinyl jacket that the speaker wore. He let his eyes fall, noting that the man's trousers were two inches shorter than they ought to have been. "Two doors down," he told the man, turning away.

A few moments later he walked past Riley's office. Riley's whimper curled into the hallway, like a bad odor. "My wife doesn't have to know about this, does she? You can say you're questioning everyone, can't you?"

Wendolyn fancied poking his head inside Riley's door. "Relax, dreg of dregs," he would say. "If the man is questioning *you*, clearly he is questioning everyone." But such a gesture might be read as banter. And banter might imply

camaraderie. And camaraderie with the likes of Riley . . .
Wendolyn shivered and continued down the hall.

He had not thought to wonder about the question that Riley
was being asked. But too soon he knew. The question was
everywhere. In the hallways, in all of his classes. In the men's
room, the dining hall, the smoker.

And the question was: Who killed Christine Rivers?

The murder of the President of the United States had been
murder removed.No one, that is, had walked in its aftermath
fearing a sniper's bullet.

The murder of Christine Rivers, though it got far less air
time, had higher ratings. In addition to the Who-Was-He? was
the Would-He-Strike-Again? But the Who-Was-He? would
have served.

Who-Was-He? enabled coeds to squeal like camp fire girls
after lights-out, the freshmen women saying that it just might
be the killer who had asked to study with them for exams, the
sophomores speculating that they had lately struggled with
him in the back seat of a Ford. Several junior girls wondered if
he was the father of the fetus they yet housed. The seniors, of
course, had diaphragms.

Who-Was-He? conferred upon many a faculty marriage the
solidity that only a wife's absolution can, for the
interrogation—like the lust of Christine Rivers—ranged the
campus. One by one the women squared their shoulders and
talked to the police: "The girl encouraged him and, after all,
he's only human. And besides, he was with me every night
last week, I swear."

Wendolyn, certainly, was never a suspect. Even when there
was no one left to question, they had not come to him. A man
who harbors murder is a changed man, aloof. But in his case,
no one noticed.

Nonetheless, Ronald Wendolyn sat with sheets of manuscript balanced on knees that quaked. He had worked on both scenes that very night, striking an adjective here, substituting one verb for another. And now he read, yet again, the detailed account of the girl's death, and of her resurrection.

In which had he been a participant? In which a maker of fiction? He imagined a policeman straddling the doorway. "Did you, Ronald Wendolyn, kill Christine Rivers?"

"I don't know, officer," he would say. "Let me check my notes."

And, in truth, he didn't know. Both accounts rang true.

To the scene in which she reappeared, he had added a coda wherein she had babbled, as he drove through the snowswept night, on and on about how someone would fix her ass and his ass too. And in that scene as it now stood, Christine Rivers had skipped from the car, lithe and live, saying what Iago said when Othello stabbed him: "I bleed, sir, but not killed."

But that, perhaps, was only what he yearned for. That, perhaps, was illusion.

For hadn't the murder scene more than witty chatter in its favor? Hadn't it her corpse, battered as he'd said it would be battered, laid where he'd said it would be laid?

Wendolyn trembled, remembering. He heard again the slap of his flesh on hers. He heard again her struggle, the sound of blood already thickening in her throat. And how he'd kept on luffing over her, even when the sounds had stopped. God, yes. The murder scene had a gaudy realism that could not but be truth.

Wendolyn walked to the fireplace and knelt before it, the pages dealing with her death in his hand. He tried to bend his fingers and winced, held them rigid again. More proof?

Even so, he couldn't cast the murder scene away. It was polished, precise. He would keep the pages intact and pray that no one ask, if ever his book was done, "Is it autobiographical?"

98

26

Lida watched him work on the button at his wrist. "What's the matter with your hand?" she asked, her skirt falling in a heap at her feet. She slid out of her pantyhose, losing her balance.

"An old injury," he told her. "The fingers don't close." He held his hand up as if for inspection. "It's something of a joke."

"A joke?" She tossed her blouse at a chair, missing by at least three feet. "I don't get it."

"A masturbatory joke." He walked over to her blouse, picked it up, shook it, and laid it across the seat.

"That's probably why I don't get it." She lay facedown on the bed, propping herself up with her elbows.

"You don't approve of masturbation?"

"In a pinch, yes."

He rolled his socks and put them inside his boots. He

looked down at her. A very nice ass. "Is your asshole absolutely cherry?" he asked.

She turned onto her side and smiled. "Yeah," she said, "and it's going to stay that way."

"You have so many silly prejudices." He sat on the bed, running his hand along her thigh. Then he leaned forward, pressing his cheek below her knee. He pulled back.

"Well," Lida explained, "you didn't give me a chance to shave."

He kissed her feet, sucked at her toes. "I assume these have never been violated"—his tongue flicked along her instep.

"Hey," Lida said, winding her fingers in his hair, "come here."

27

Wendolyn pushed toward his car, just short of breaking into a run. He was eager to escape the wind. He liked the cold when he was ready for it, but today had promised unseasonable highs, and he had dressed accordingly. Now the wind pressed against his chest and screamed in his ears. He turned his collar up, but it did no good.

He closed the door of the car behind him, feeling sheltered. He was glad to have left the meeting early. The temperature was dropping fast.

He had written some good notes. A member of the Student Government Association had addressed the faculty. She spoke of strengthening student participation in college affairs. Wendolyn imagined her in wide-eyed struggle. Her opponent, a rather ordinary chap, something like Paul Riley.

"We should all join hands," she was saying, "to make this campus . . . "

The assailant twisted her fingers, one by one, until each had broken.

The point of his pencil snapped. He creased the sheets, put them in his pocket, and left.

The car made a slow, grinding sound. He switched it off, then began anew. Eventually, he knew, it would start.

The light from the streetlamp was blocked, suddenly. He turned and saw a figure stooping beside the car, peering inside. He rolled the window down.

"Having trouble?"

"No." Wendolyn was impatient. "It will start. I'm having a new battery installed in the morning."

"I don't think it's your battery," the intruder said. "Sounds more like ignition trouble."

"Thank you. It *will* start." Just then, it did.

"Can you give me a ride?" he shouted at Wendolyn.

"Sorry, no. I don't go very far."

"Anything will help. It's getting kind of cold out here."

The car stalled just as he prepared to pull away. Wendolyn turned the key again, but the sound was weaker. Then weaker still.

"I'll give you a push. We can kick-start it."

"I don't understand." He had never been able to impose order on mechanical things, a shortcoming which frequently led to inconvenience.

"Shit, man, where've you been? Take the brake off, put the thing in gear, and when it starts to roll, let the clutch out. It'll start."

Wendolyn took the brake off, put the car in gear, and, when it started to roll, released the clutch. There was a brief sputter, then nothing. He turned the key again, but this time there was no sound whatsoever.

"Hey"—the man yanked the door open—"I'll tell you what. You push. *I'll* start it."

Wendolyn stared at him, uncertain.

"I'm not gonna steal your car. What do I look like, Jack the Ripper?"

Wendolyn stepped out and the man slid in, flinging a canvas satchel into the back seat. "You won't have to push it very far," he called, "there's enough of a grade."

He waited for Wendolyn halfway down the hill. But he didn't get out. He eased over into the passenger seat, keeping his foot on the gas pedal as long as he could. "Don't let it stall now," he said.

"Thanks very much," Wendolyn said, pulling onto the main road.

"How long does it take for your heater to get going?"

"Too long," Wendolyn said. "I'm afraid we'll be there before it gets warm."

"That's too bad." He gestured at the radio. "What kind of stations you get around here?"

"You aren't local?" Wendolyn was surprised.

"I'm nothin'. I'm just on the move."

"That must be difficult."

No reply.

They reached the foot of Wendolyn's driveway. He stopped the car. Then he reconsidered. "I can drive you into town if you like."

"This your place?"

"Yes."

"Looks pretty fancy."

"I have a lot of work to do," Wendolyn said. "Shall I take you or not?"

"Wife waiting for you?"

"Yes," Wendolyn said.

"She always sit in the dark?" The man laughed.

"I can drop you *here*"—Wendolyn's voice was like steel—"or I can take you into town. Whichever you prefer."

"Who does your work around the place?" The man seemed not to notice Wendolyn's tone.

"I do."

"Like that mailbox?"

Wendolyn had wired it to the post that the headlights illuminated. The wind had torn at it until it dangled by a single thread. "What is it you want?" he asked. "Money?"

"I could use some. In exchange for odd jobs." He looked over at Wendolyn. "You give me some chow, a place to spend the night, and I'll spend all day tomorrow fixing things up."

"Like the mailbox."

"Yeah, like that. Maybe even the car. I'm, you know, handy."

"I don't really have a spare room," he said.

"Look, friend. I spent last night in a bus station."

Wendolyn's car hesitated up the drive.

"Better turn it around," the stranger directed.

"Why?"

"Because you might have to kick it in the morning."

"Oh, yes." Wendolyn did so.

❦

"Not bad." The satchel thudded to the floor. "By the way, my name's Jack." He stood with his hands on his hips, surveying the room.

"I am"—he paused, seeking distance—"Dr. Wendolyn."

"Yeah? Figures. How many operations a day does it take to pay for a place like this?"

"No, no"—Wendolyn laughed—"not *that* kind of doctor. I teach at the college."

Jack looked puzzled. "If you say so," he said.

Wendolyn had never created a lower-class character. He had never heeded any for the length of time it would require. He would remedy that. "Come on, Jack"—he walked back toward the kitchen—"I have a very nice cheese . . . "

104

"Jesus Christ," Jack said, "what could be nice about a cheese?"

℣

Wendolyn awakened. Such a queer dream. Of Jack, wearing gaudy undershorts, coming out of the bathroom. The yellow light behind him, then gone. The sound of someone else in the room, breathing. Then the kitchen. Jack, in the kitchen after dinner. His belch, loud, deliberate, even forced. The scrape of his chair on the kitchen floor. But not a scrape. A squeal. Like the squeal of brakes in the student parking lot. Then the sound of glass breaking.

He stared into the darkness of the room. Something unusual about it. Something shallow. He moved to the window. A pale beam of light striking out at the sky.

He groped for his trousers. Not there. He found his bathrobe and, not bothering to tie it closed, moved downstairs.

He stood beside the sofa and listened. Nothing. He called Jack's name. Then he reached down to confirm what he already knew.

He went back to the bedroom and crouched by the open window. The light still there. Voices, coming closer.

℣

They hammered on the door.

Wendolyn shivered in the shaft of cold air, but didn't move. Had he, now, after all this time, been uncovered? And had Jack been the instrument of it, had Jack read the manuscript, recognized the girl, the setting?

"Who'd ya expect to answer?" one of the men was shouting.

"I dunno. He could have a wife or something."

"He didn't have no wife. I'm tellin' ya, my sister's kid was

105

takin' his class. He was a weirdo. Lived up here all by his lonesome."

"Look, Charlie, it don't hurt to check."

He heard one of the men walking along the side of the house. "Hey!" It was the one called Charlie. "This door over here's open."

"I ain't goin' in there."

"We're just gonna use the phone."

"I don't wanna go in there."

"Well, stand out here, then, and freeze your fucking ass off. We gotta report this, and I can't see walkin' all the way back to town."

"Whad'ya mean, walk? That truck will roll."

"Sure, that truck will roll. And then they'll nail us for leavin' the scene."

"Shit." He gave in.

Wendolyn crept to the top of the stairs and tensed. His own breathing seemed inordinately loud. He could feel each beat of his heart.

"Not a bad place," one of the men said.

He couldn't tell which one. Then he heard the dial of the telephone turning.

"Listen, Matt? . . . Charlie. Hey, listen, we had an accident. . . . Naw, we're okay. But, hey. You better send some of your boys out here, because the other guy is not okay. He's mashed up pretty good."

Silence. Who? Wendolyn wondered.

"Naw, worse than that. Like, his own mother wouldn't recognize him, you know? Yeah, I mean dead. Jesus, what do you think I mean? Dead, man, d-e-a-d, dead."

"Tell him it wasn't our fault," the other man said.

"That Wendolyn guy. Sure you do. Wendolyn, the schoolmarm? No, I'm sure. We got his wallet with all his ID, you know, credit cards. the works. And it happened right here. Right *here*. Yeah, we're at his place now. Okay, meet you down there."

The schoolmarm almost giggled. But then he remembered the words "mashed up" and regained his composure.

"It wasn't our fault," the other man repeated.

"Huh? Naw, I got Bill with me . . . *I* was . . . Naw, Christ. Look, we're out in the truck salting the road, see? And the Wendolyn guy, he pulls right out like we wasn't there. I mean right out. But that's not all. Then he stops, Just *stops*. And he's in one of these dinky little cars. Foreign job, you know? You could put what's left of it in your pocket. We hit him broadside. Couldn't help it." He laughed gutturally. "Sure, you can send an ambulance. It won't do no good, but you can send one."

He hung up. "Ambulance!" he said. "Better they should send a sponge."

Wendolyn heard the liquor cabinet swing open, then Bill's voice. "Aw, shit, Charlie, put that back. We got sixty bucks out of the guy's wallet. What more do you want?"

Wendolyn could not make out Charlie's reply.

When they were in the driveway, he went into the bathroom and urinated. He reached for the handle. But no. He couldn't flush the toilet. They might hear.

He stumbled over something. Clothing. He stooped and ran his hands over the fabric. Not his own. Jack's.

He slipped into the trousers. Just a bit too large. Not noticeably large, he guessed, but large in the way that ready-made trousers might be. The shirt, on the other hand, fit him perfectly. He had an eerie feeling, standing there in the clothes of a dead man. But it seemed just, in a way. Poor mashed-up Jack had thought to rob him, credit cards, the works. He shrugged. He felt around the bathroom floor. The canvas satchel.

ᴗ

What would he need? Money. He went to the bedroom closet, hoping Jack had not been there first. Good. He would have to count it in daylight, but there was enough, he was certain.

He could not take a chance on the typewriter. Surely its sound, too, would carry. He laid a sheet of paper on his desk and coaxed it flat.

He lamented the ball-point pen his fingers found—standard departmental issue—as much as he lamented the generosity fate had imposed upon him.

Ah, well. He dated the document some six months earlier.

Two witnesses, he calculated, would suffice. Charlie and Bill. He invented Charles Tremont, who scrawled his name illegibly. And William Ryder, who had a pinched, girlish hand and who made his final R rather like an N.

Wendolyn folded his last will and testament and placed it in the box where the money had been.

What else? His manuscript, of course. He rolled it and forced it into the satchel. Then he placed the bag and Jack's worn jacket beside the kitchen door.

He stood in the darkness imagining this room, the rooms beyond. Would he be tempted to return here one bright day? Return, as legend had it, to the scene of his crime? No. He would ensure against any such urge.

He retreated to his desk, found yet another sheet. On it he wrote: *I, Ronald Wendolyn, did murder Christine Rivers.* Too dull? What might he have said? That she ceased upon the midnight with no pain? That he had taken her till death did them part? Bah. *I, Ronald Wendolyn, did murder Christine Rivers* was to the point. It had a certain Anglo-Saxon ring, unfrilled. It would do.

108

He folded the paper and groped his way to the fireplace. He slid the sheet back along the mantel's ledge.

Who would find it? One who, as his will stipulated, would hold the Wendolyn Chair, live in Wendolyn House. One who would receive the Wendolyn Professorship and—if the scholar was tidy—the Wendolyn secret.

He listened again. A siren sounded in the distance. He went into the bathroom and waited.

When the wail was close enough and loud enough, he gave his last peformance in the role of Ronald Wendolyn. He grabbed the handle and, with a flourish, flushed.

His toes and fingers ached with cold, but he went on. The ground was frozen, with no give. Like walking on rock.

Daylight had barely begun. Ahead and to the left, he saw a flicker of neon, then a steady white light. That would be Obie Hardison's service station.

Good. It meant that he had bypassed the town and was at least a good three miles south of it.

There were two gas stations near the college. He had only been to this one twice in the eight years he had been there. He wouldn't, he reasoned, be able to select Hardison from a group of local residents. Why, then, should Hardison recognize him?

Anyway, he would have to risk it. He was too cold to go on.

He opened the door, and the old man, warming his hands over a small gas stove, turned. "Mornin'," he said cheerily.

"Good morning."

"What happened? Car break down?"

"Out of gas," he improvised.

"I can't drive you back," Hardison said, "until my helper gets here. Can't leave the place untended."

"That's all right."

"I'll have some coffee here in a minute," Hardison went on, walking over to a hot plate and looking down into a small

aluminum pot. "It'll be a few minutes. I just opened up. What
are you, traveling through?"

Safe.

"You must have walked a ways," Hardison said. "Here."
He wheeled a chair in front of the heater. "Set yourself down."

"I wonder," he asked, "if I might use your men's room."

Hardison grunted. "Back there."

❦

He counted his money first. Five hundred and thirty-four
dollars in bills. Probably more than two dollars in change. He
would have to be careful but, yes, he would manage.

He sat on the commode, took the manuscript out, and balanced it in his hands. Yes, there was enough. He laid it on the
floor and watched the pages curl, as if alive.

He scraped his fingers on the bottom of the satchel and
produced three cards. He dealt them onto the concrete, as if
playing solitaire. Three driving permits, each bearing a different name.

The first was a District of Columbia permit issued to Jackson
Robert Wisniewski. It carried Jack's photograph, in color, in
the upper-right-hand corner. He tore it in two.

The second card identified John Robert Wilkins Bishop. A
Delaware license.

The third bore the name of Jackson R.W. Bishop. It was from
Pennsylvania.

He deliberated for a moment, then tore the Delaware card in
half. He slipped the Pennsylvania license back into the
satchel.

Jackson R.W. Bishop washed his hands and rejoined Obie
Hardison.

❦

"Which way you headed?" Hardison asked. He was taking
change from the register.

110

"South."

"Well, I tell you. Maybe you can get this guy out here to take you."

Bishop squinted. He could not see beyond his own reflection in the plate-glass window. "Who is it?" he asked. "Someone from the town?"

"Nope. Guy's got Canadian plates." He frowned. "And Canadian money."

Bishop started outside to solicit a ride.

"Wait up," Hardison called. "You don't want to forget your gas." He brandished a can with a separate nozzle.

"Oh, yes, thank you."

"Five-dollar deposit on the can," Hardison told him. He laid the can and the nozzle on the counter and held out his hand.

"I'd like to buy the can."

"What's that?"

"Buy it. Keep it. I'd rather not drive back this way." He put the nozzle into his satchel.

"Ten dollars?" Hardison was tentative. "Gas and all," he added.

"Fine." He selected a bill and handed it over.

"Shit," Hardison said out loud, watching the car, with Jackson R.W. Bishop in the passenger seat, pull out of the station and onto the highway. "I probably could have got fifteen." He crumpled up the money and put it in his pants pocket.

111

28

"It's so crazy," Diana said, brushing her hair in front of the mirror. It crackled with static electricity, falling slowly, resisting gravity. "I don't know anything about you, really."

"Nonsense," Allen told her. "You know everything about me. My base ambition. My cavalier indifference to the law . . ."

"I mean the standard things."

"Ah!" He bowed from the waist. "Student of Christ Church, Oxford. Jury Professor of English at—where was it? Yes, at Leeds. Before that, lecturer at Queen's University, Belfast. Three years ago, seduced to New Hampshire, where the esteemed Wendolyn Chair waited. I didn't stress any of this earlier, of course, because I want you to love me for myself and not for the prestigious posts I've held." He ahemed.

Diana laughed, meeting his eyes in the mirror. Wait until Lida met him. Wouldn't Lida *die*? She caught her breath. "Will you be at the MLA?" she asked. The meeting of the Modern Language Association would be held in New York, two months away. She and Lida would go together. "Or is that too pedestrian a place for you?"

"I will be there. I'll be giving a very pedestrian paper."

"And afterwards?"

"My very dignified colleague, Riley, promised to line everyone in the department up with—let me see, how did he phrase that? Oh, yes, 'a few cute tricks.' "

"I don't believe he said that."

"I swear it!" Allen walked toward her, growing serious. "But, Diana," he said, "the MLA is long away. Surely I'll see you before then?"

29

"Oh, hey," Lida said, examining her eyes in the bathroom mirror, "do you mind if I use your toothbrush?" She held it under the faucet and ran a stream of water over the bristles.

He had already brushed his teeth. He would buy another. "No," he said, "go right ahead." He walked back into the bedroom and finished dressing.

She came out, wiping the corners of her mouth with her fingers. She was naked but for the towel draped around her shoulders. She wore no makeup. She looked older than she had last night.

"I know," she said, "I look awful."

"Yes," he said, darkening his voice, "awful." He thought of one of his heroes who, in a similar circumstance, had said, "You've had me. Now, leave." He reached for the ends of the towel and held them. "What will you do today?" he asked. He would think of her, later, doing whatever it was.

"Loaf," she said.

No visual image came to mind. He tried again. "And tonight?"

"Oh, I'll probably go to the theater. With Diana."

"And tomorrow?"

"Tomorrow the grind starts again. Not classes, but meetings. Oh, God, how I hate meetings."

"Ah, yes, meetings. How well I remember."

"What time is it?" she asked. "Do you know?"

"No." He dropped the towel and kissed her lightly. "You smell of toothpaste," he said, wrinkling his nose.

"So do you." She reached down and pressed her hands against his trousers.

"No, don't," he said, taking her hands. "I just wanted to kiss you."

The hotel restaurant had not yet opened for breakfast. They went across the street to a Howard Johnson's.

"What are you chuckling about?" he asked.

"The thought of the mighty Duvivier in a Howard Johnson's."

"That is a funny thought." He sipped at his juice. He pushed it aside. "This is too sweet."

"I'll drink it," Lida offered, reaching across for it.

"You're very lucky," he said, "to be able to loaf today. I wish I could loaf." He italicized the word, played with it. It was one he had never used.

"Don't you, ever?"

"I don't think so. No. I don't think I ever have. Does it require a bucolic setting?"

"No," she said, sliding deep into the corner of the booth. "In fact, we're loafing now."

"We are?"

"Can't you tell?" She closed her eyes. "What about you?"

she asked. "What will you do today?"

"Fly to New York. Settle in. Get everything done as quickly as possible. And then go back abroad."

"Sounds great," she said sadly.

He narrowed his eyes, measuring her words, her manner. "I may have to stay a bit longer. To write another scene. I'm not sure."

"A scene for the movie?"

"Yes."

"And will it be a murder?" The life had returned to her voice. "I love your murders."

He looked swiftly across the table at her. A stern look.

She didn't seem to care. "My favorite," she said, pausing to swallow, "was the one in Spain. The one with the kids and the costumes and the donkeys, remember?"

That one had been his agent's idea. He had only complied. "Mmm," he said, cutting the crust from his toast.

"Hey, tell me. How did you happen to come to Washington in the first place?" she asked, widening her eyes and sitting upright. "You never told me."

"It was"—he shrugged—"just an extraordinary mix-up in my travel arrangements, that's all."

"God!" Lida said. "Which airline was it? No kidding, I'd like to send them a bouquet of roses!"

He smiled across at her. "You've never told me," he said, "just what it was that prompted your letter."

"I don't remember," Lida said, "and that's the truth."

※

He held her coat. "Is there a clock?" he asked, turning his head to see. Lida's smile sagged. But then he said, "I have a bit of time." Did he sound glad?

She slid her arms into the sleeves. He pulled at her collar, then let his hands rest on her shoulders. His breath brushed her neck. She felt her hair stir slightly. His hands drifted to her hips, pressing against the thick wool folds.

"God," she said, "I've been liberated for so long, I'd forgotten what this was like."

He laughed, guiding her toward the door, reaching past her to push it open. "Yes, it's very sexy. And socially acceptable."

"I'm serious," Lida said.

"I am, too."

They crossed the street and wandered through a complex of shops. Lida watched their reflection in every plate-glass window, as though she were watching a film.

"Do you approve of what you see?" he asked.

"Actually, no. I was wishing I were younger. With a cuter nose. And with long blond hair that would sweep along the pavement."

He wished she hadn't said that about her nose. Christine Rivers had had a cute nose. "How old are you?" he asked.

"Thirty-five," she said, thinking that she should have lied.

"You're a child. A mere child."

"How old are you?"

Ronald Wendolyn would have been forty-six. But when he had assumed the Jackson R.W. Bishop identity, he had dropped two years. "I'm forty-four," he said, "but I feel older."

"How old do you feel?"

"Forty-six."

They stood in front of a bookstore. Several volumes were propped up for display. "There's your new book," she said.

"Mmmm,"he said absently.

"Hey, did you read that?" She pointed to *Blood and Money*.

"I don't read," he said with a trace of irritation.

"We're open now"—a woman leaned out at them—"if you'd like to come inside."

Duvivier looked at Lida. "Yes," Lida said, "let's."

He followed her through the doorway. The sales clerk stationed herself alongside some shelves to the right. She smiled at them approvingly. Lida walked to the remainder

117

counter and began sifting through some battered hardcovers reduced to a dollar apiece.

"Oh, no," Duvivier groaned. "You're not one of those."

"Now you know," Lida said, laughing back at him.

He walked toward the back of the store. "Look," he called, waving an oversized paperback, *The Illustrated Manual of Sex Therapy*.

Lida dropped the mystery she'd selected and came rushing toward him. "Is that one of those Sprinkle-coconut-on-your-nipples-and-toast-them-lightly-under-the-broiler jobs?"

"No," he announced, flipping it open and reading aloud. "It's one of those A-negative-response-of-sensate-focus-on-the-part-of-either-partner-is-an-obstacle-to-further-therapy jobs."

"*Of* sensate focus? Is that what it says?" Lida asked.

He looked back at the page. "Oh, sorry, 'A negative response *to* sensate focus.' "

"Can I *help* you?" The woman advanced on them, her tone scolding. She snatched the book away.

"Shall I buy it for you?" he asked Lida. "A sort of farewell present?"

The clerk mustered a smile. She stood, ready to relinquish the book.

"Do I need it?" Lida asked him.

He turned to the woman. "Thank you, madam," he said, "but no."

118

30

Lida waited for the left-turn signal to appear. She felt changed. In soft focus. Like a perfume commercial. "You touch Masumi," she said out loud, "Masumi touches you." When the green arrow appeared, the car in front of her sputtered and died. The soft focus dissolved.

"You bozo!" she yelled, backing, whipping to the right, and squealing around the bend. She had barely gone a block when a cop stepped into her lane, gesturing.

"Me?" she mimed, pulling to the curb.

She rolled her window down. "Please don't give me a ticket," she said. "I've got diarrhea and I was trying to get to a toilet."

"That's what they all say, lady." He poised pencil over pad.

"I don't believe that," Lida countered.

"Radar says you were doing forty-two in a twenty-five-mile-zone." A singsong recitation. "I'll need your driver's license and your registration."

"I have two tickets in Maryland, and if I get another one now, they'll probably take my license away." She didn't mention traffic court and her no-show the night before. She fished through her purse and found the license. She didn't have the registration. "And forty-two isn't fast," she said, handing him the card.

"On Connecticut Avenue, lady, forty-two is fast." He walked back to a police car that she hadn't noticed before. She watched in the mirror as he leaned inside. When he came back, he was writing.

"It didn't feel fast," she said.

He handed her the ticket and a little slip of paper.

"What's this?" she asked.

"If you go to traffic school, you won't get any points and you won't have to pay the ticket. And, *wait* a minute"—he held up his hand to keep her from interrupting— "the offense won't be reported to Maryland."

"Thanks," she said. He hadn't remembered the registration.

"And, lady, better get yourself some Kaopectate." He grinned. "It's a heck of a lot cheaper than . . ." Lida followed his gaze. He was looking at a stack of parking tickets on her dashboard, some bright orange, others sun-weathered into a creamy beige. "You know," he said, "I could impound your car for those."

Lida pulled out her best springer-spaniel look. "Impound? For parking tickets?"

"How many have you got?" He held out his hand and Lida gathered them and deposited them there. "Seven!" he said. "Hey, they're gonna get you. I'm surprised there wasn't a warrant out on you when I called in."

"A warrant? You must be kidding."

"Look. I'm not kidding. Technically, I could impound your car. I won't. But someone is going to if you don't pay these.

They don't mess around with these things." He handed the tickets back to her.

Lida pulled out her checkbook. "Here. I'll pay you for them right now. How much? Then you can go back to headquarters a hero."

He looked around. "Come on, put that away. It looks bad, you know, me standing here and you flashing your checkbook." He pushed her hands back inside the window. "Just get out of here, okay?"

"Okay," Lida said, "you had your chance." She slid the gearshift lever into first. "I never thought I'd say this to a cop, but you're a nice guy. Even if you did call me 'lady.' "

He stood back and grinned again. "Yeah, I know," he said, "I'm a peach."

The phone. It was probably Diana. Good. She couldn't wait to tell her.

"Lida, listen..." Diana's voice was backed by highway sounds.

"Where are you?" Lida shouted.

"On my way home," she said.

"On your *way*? We're supposed to go to the theater tonight."

"I won't make it," Diana said.

"Shit."

"Listen, I can't talk," Diana said. "You'll have to go over to Bill's and pick up my kids."

"Me? Are you crazy?"

"Please! I've been trying to call him, and the line was busy, and finally I had the operator check and she said it was out of order. Please. I told him I'd be there."

"I don't know where he lives," Lida said.

"I can give you directions. Will you?"

❧

Lida turned off the beltway at the Great Falls exit. The homes were a cut above average, but Lida disapproved of them anyway. Damn. Why did Bill expect Diana to drive from New Hampshire and still come all the way out here to get the kids? Damn.

She swerved into his driveway, her wheels gouging the lawn. She stalked to the door.

"Well, well, *well*," he said, "who are *you*?"

"Can it, buster," Lida answered. "I'm your ex-wife's best friend."

"Oh," he said flatly, "where is she?"

"Detained. Parting was such sweet sorrow and all that. Where are they?"

He looked blank.

"The kids," she explained.

"Soccer game."

"Do you know that your phone isn't working?"

"It's off the hook," he said, stepping back. "Come on in." His eyes moved over her body. "So you're the famous Lida," he said.

Lida wished she'd closed a few more buttons on her chambray workshirt. Or worn baggier jeans. But it was too late now. She put her hands on her hips, braving it out. "And you're the famous Bill."

"Has Diana told you about me?"

"Enough." She tossed her head.

"What has she said?" He knew he was on safe ground. Diana never said anything bad about anybody.

"Not much. I know that you're a premature ejaculator."

He opened his mouth like a goldfish.

"Or . . . wait a minute. Maybe you're the impotent one. I

122

get everyone's ex-es all mixed up."

"I am not." He said it like a little boy.

"No?" Lida advanced on him. "Prove it." She reached for his belt buckle and undid it.

"What the hell are you doing?" he said, trying to close it.

"Come on, prove it. Get it up." Lida lunged for his zipper, as if to pull it down.

"You're insane," he said, reaching first for his fly, then his belt, then abandoning both to catch her hands. "Get out of here."

Lida laughed at him. "Diana wants her children delivered promptly at eight. And make sure you've fed them. Royally." At the doorway she turned. "By the way, sweet lips. I was only fooling."

She drove off feeling that she'd just put a notch in Diana's column.

31

Diana was surprised to find the house dark. She went inside, flipping all the light switches along the way.

The air was thick and musty. She opened the door to the patio and let the cold night wind wash in.

She sat at the kitchen counter and dialed Bill's number. The phone rang this time, but there was no answer.

She called Lida. "Are my kids at your place?" she asked.

"No. Hey, hello. No. Bill insisted on bringing them home."

"He *insisted*?"

"Yeah. See, they weren't in when I got there, and he had planned to take them out to dinner . . ."

"You're kidding."

"No."

"Lida, did you *ask* him to do this?"

"Ask him? No, I didn't ask him. Diana, listen, I have a ton of stuff to tell you. You won't believe it!"

"Oh, wait, I think I hear them."

"Diana," Lida said.

"I'll have to call you back."

"Wait. Let's go somewhere, like a Chinese place. I just *have* to talk to you."

"Chinese!" She fought to keep the anger from her voice, but it was there, she knew. "Lida, I've been driving all day long. How can you expect me to do that and then go out to a Chinese restaurant? I haven't even *seen* my children! Now, I've *got* to hang up."

But Lida hung up before she did. Oh, well, Lida would just have to understand, that's all. She would talk to her tomorrow. It would be all right.

The front door slammed. Then it opened, ricocheted off the door stop, and slammed again. She ran in and hugged each of the boys in turn.

"Where's your father?" she asked.

"Aw, he had to get back," said her middle son, Tim.

"Boy," Eddie, her youngest, said. "It really stinks in here."

The troupe moved past her. Her eldest tossed his jacket to the floor and stretched in front of the patio door. "That air sure feels good," he said.

Upstairs, Timmy had begun to play the stereo. The angry chords of Jimi Hendrix filled the house.

Eddie rooted through the refrigerator. "Is this cupcake still good?" he asked, dangling a plastic bag.

"I thought you just had dinner." She put her arms around him. He was taller than she.

"I did. Hey, come on, Mom. You're gonna smash my cupcake."

Diana imagined herself snatching it, Baggie and all, in her fist. She would squeeze until chunks of devil's food curled through the sundered seams. And Eddie, staring at her knuckles, would fall to his knees, repentant. "I'll get you a plate," she told her son, but he had already smeared the cupcake into his mouth.

"Stale," he said, handing her the soiled bag and sauntering off to join his brothers.

Diana sat down at the kitchen table, rubbing her knuckles, twisting her ring.

"So this is motherhood," Lida had once observed. "Matching socks and settling disputes and looking for their *TV Guide* at half-hour intervals. Jesus, you can have it."

The boys took turns doing chores, of course. Diana had seen to that. But always she had to press them into service, sometimes wheedling, occasionally bribing, often shouting. And after one or another of them had, say, cleaned the kitchen, she would always find a congealed lump of something on the countertop. A sort of token. A way of saying "We need you, Mom."

A few weeks ago she had been going into the powder room just off the downstairs hall: Eddie was at the sink, desultorily washing the dishes, while Lida sat reading at the dining-room table.

"Hey, Mom," Eddie shouted, "I can't get this pot clean."

She was about to tell him to leave it. That she would do it later.

But Lida answered him. "Throw it away," Lida said.

"Throw this pot away?" Eddie had whined. "Are you crazy?"

"Well, if *you* can't get it clean," Lida had said, "how do you expect your mother to get it clean? Throw it away."

Diana had lingered in the bathroom, wondering what the outcome would be. Later, she noted the pot had been scoured to a shine.

Her children hated Lida, of course. They would contrive sore throats and sprained ankles whenever they caught wind of any plans that she and Lida had made. Diana always gave in.

"Sore throat, my ass," Lida would say.

But Diana, firm in the belief that even a phony sore throat

was a legitimate plea for her attention, would tell her, "I can't go, Lida, and that's that."

And Lida would slam the door behind her, or hurl the receiver into its cradle. It had happened a hundred times.

Now Diana was weary of the contest.

It was Lida who continually ranted about the boys' demands. But not, Diana felt, because Lida was attempting to protect her from their infringement. No. Because the demands of the children frequently conflicted with Lida's own demands.

She would not call Lida, damn it. She would do nothing. She would spend the entire evening doing absolutely nothing.

"I'm feeling sick," she told her children, musing that she should have said, "I'm feeling healthy." "I'm going up to my room and I'm going to lock the door. I don't want any phone calls. I don't want any interruptions. And turn everything down. I don't want to hear *Kojak* or Jimi Hendrix or any arguments. Is that clear?"

They looked at her and then at each other.

Diana went upstairs, relieved.

Diana opened her eyes and listened for the steady, whistling sound that Allen had made as he slept. But there was silence.

She sat up. She was still wearing the corduroy slacks she had driven home in. And the blouse. And the sweater. She pulled the blouse free and reached under it to unclasp her brassiere, straining forward as she did so to read the eerie numerals on the clock. It was, she thought, just after five.

She tried to will herself to stand and walk toward the shower. Get an early start. But there was no need for that. No classes today. Nor had the two committees on which she served planned to wrangle. It was a rare gift, this day. She could lean back against her pillow and court her memory.

Allen. His thick wrists and fingers. That wiry hair bristling everywhere. The pocket of warmth that his body made, wide enough for her to curl inside. And the wonderful sound of him there beside her.

I slept with him, she thought. I literally *slept* with him. With Lou—or with anyone married—that would not have been likely. Not without lies and complex logistics.

She was glad, now, to have settled for a corned-beef sandwich that morning with Lou. Glad to have waited for Allen.

Diana laughed out loud. Lord, she thought, wouldn't Lida make fun of me now? She would say I was thinking like a virgin.

32

Lida yawned and stretched and switched the radio on. It was Purcell, *The Fairy Queen*. The part where the woman sings: "I will never, never, never never never . . . "

Lida thought about calling Diana, but then remembered hanging up on her last night. It was just as well. How could she explain the difference between *this* one-night stand and all the others?

And there was a difference. She hadn't figured it out yet, but there was.

She sang along with the voice on the radio: "I will never, never, never never never . . . "

She knelt beside the bed and lifted the dust ruffle. She slid her hand about until she found the little barbells, five-pound weights that she used occasionally to postpone what she had termed the Lucille Felton jiggle.

Lida held the weights to either side of her body and made

ever-widening circles. First one way, then the other. She thought of Duvivier, off in some New York hotel room, doing similar calisthenics. There was no mistaking the way his skin stretched over long hard muscle. He had worked at it.

Lida smiled, touching her toes and leaving the weights there on the floor. She would leave early, she decided, and jog around the park before all that Brady State garbage.

Duvivier stood in the oral-hygiene section of the drugstore, absentmindedly holding a plastic container of dental floss.

"You want that, Mac?" a clerk addressed him.

"Mmm? No. Just looking." He replaced it on the shelf, turning to the row upon row of toothbrushes on display. There were green ones. Blue ones. Yellow ones. Red ones.

His own was opaque gray.

He thought, then, of Lida's mouth, of its serpent-deep hollows. His hand shuddered along the column headings: Soft. Medium. Firm. Extra-firm.

"You want one of them brushes, Mac?" The clerk was still at his side. He had to ask the question a second time before Duvivier could answer.

"No," he said.

When Lida got to the campus she discovered Mrs. Semple, the public-information officer, waiting for her. As far as Lida knew, the woman's first name was Mrs. At least, that was how she signed her name: Mrs. Semple—in a careful backhand stroke. She was the sort of woman who would make eyes out of the O's in "look" and think it clever. Her mission today was to interview Lida for the *All-College Newsletter*.

"What does your husband do?" Mrs. Semple asked.

"I'm not married."

"Oh." The woman flushed. "I'm, oh, I'm so sorry."

"I'll live."

"I mean, most people are, and so I always ask, you know, 'What does your husband do?' or 'What does your wife do?' . . ." She waved the ball-point pen about as if she were sinking and that gesture might help keep her afloat.

"It's okay."

"It's a natural assumption. But, of course, don't get me wrong. There's nothing *wrong* with being single. Sometimes I wish I were single myself." She had a hollow laugh, just short of a whinny.

"Could we get on with this?" Lida said. "My lonely hearts club meets in an hour."

Mrs. Semple cleared her throat. "What's your pet peeve?" she asked.

Lida's mind ran the course. Men who say "Little Boy's Room." Men who say "Head." Men who say "Can." Men who wash after sex. "Oh, I don't know," she said, "I'm pretty easygoing."

"There must be some little thing." She sang the word "little" as though speaking to a child.

"Oh, I guess people who get in the express line with more than ten items."

Semple laid the pen down. "Yes!" she said with feeling. "Don't you just *hate* that!"

"Yes, I do."

Semple picked up the pen and, pressing very hard, wrote it down.

The interview with Mrs. Semple had taken longer than Lida had expected. That meant she might have to postpone her call to Seare and Jolly. Ah, well, she would still have time to search out the Wendolyn book.

She pushed open the library door and went to the little

machines that served as a card catalog. She smiled at á sign someone had taped to one of them. "This machine is temporarily in working order."

They had been Jerry's idea. He was big on technology. She, as part of the Library Committee, had voted to adopt them. "Come on, Lida," he had urged her. "The kids'll love them. They're just like pinball machines."

Lida thought about the gadget that monitored his heartbeat. She should have known, damn it. She should have known.

She peered at the telescreen. God, they had it! She copied the call number and proceeded to the stacks.

There were voices on the other side of the column. One was LaChelle's. The other, Jame Jackson's. Lida peeked across the top of a row of books.

LaChelle was putting it to him. "You don't wanna love me, boy," she drawled, "well, kiss mah ass."

"That's the spirit, LaChelle," Lida called through the stacks.

"Say, what?" Jame said.

Lida tucked the Wendolyn book in her purse and walked past the desk without stopping at the checkout. "Well, kiss mah ass," she chanted, going downstairs to the pay phone.

She fished out some coins and did a brief review. Vermouth. And lemon. And Carol Bradley. That was easy enough.

Duvivier was right. It *was* more fun this way.

33

The phone in Lida's office rang several times. Just as Diana was about to hang up, one of the students answered.

She had just missed Lida, it seemed. Lida had been there talking to Mrs. Semple, and then she had gathered up her things and gone.

Diana grinned at the thought of Lida and Mrs. Semple together. In conversation with the other members of the department, Lida referred to Semple as "The Missus." When speaking to Diana alone, however, Lida called her "that douche bag." She could hardly wait to hear Lida tell of it.

She transferred her call to the departmental office and found that Lida was in a meeting. The Library Committee, the secretary thought.

Oh, God. No wonder Lida had wanted to talk last night. Jerry Felton was on the Library Committee and Lida hadn't seen him—or any other man—since that awful business in the hospital.

She wished now that she had phoned Lida as she'd promised.

Maybe she would go to Lida's. Yes. She would do the grocery shopping, and then, as soon as she'd put everything away, she'd drive over there.

34

The Library Committee meeting was in session when Lida got there. Jerry, a stack of papers on the arm of his desk chair, was gesturing at a man to his right, a florid specimen, complete with beer belly and, Lida noted, white socks.

The subject at hand was security. Jerry had located a company that produced a device designed to stop the theft of library materials. White Socks was the sales representative of that company.

"They pass through this invisible beam," Jerry was saying, excited, "and if they've stolen anything, a buzzer sounds."

"And then," Lida asked, "does a little chopper come down and sever their hand, or what?"

Jerry's laughter was halting, more like a cough. "I've researched this very carefully, Lida," he said.

"I'm sure you have, Jer. I know how thorough you are."

Halfway into the presentation, Lida pulled the stolen Wendolyn book from her purse and began to read.

White Socks passed out brochures and then went on to recite the copy aloud. "Are there any questions?" he asked when he had finished.

"Yeah," Lida said, putting the Wendolyn back into her purse. "How much does this thing cost?"

"Well," he said, "the device alone would come to . . ."—he scratched some figures onto a pad—"approximately seven thousand dollars."

"What about installing it?" Lida said.

"Well, the installation depends on a number of factors, any one of which could work to reduce or inflate the cost structure—"

"Rock bottom," Lida interrupted, "how much?"

"Rock bottom," he said, "I don't know."

"I have a feeling"—Lida looked around the room—"that we're talking about spending our entire allotment." The Library Committee had twelve thousand dollars to work with, less than half the money it had requested.

"I have a feeling," she went on, catching the cadence of Martin Luther King, on the steps of the Lincoln Memorial, maybe, "that we won't have any money left to buy books. Books!"

She turned to the chairman of her department, who also served on the committee. His name was Lance. Lida had once confided to Diana her suspicion that he'd changed it from Tyrone, better to serve as the black community's answer to Norman Mailer. "I have a feeling that if we wanted to stage a reading of the novel that Lance has been working on"—she saw Lance's teeth appear in his corner of the room—"we wouldn't have the funds to publicize it. At least, not the way it would deserve to be publicized." Lida begged the Muses to forgive her.

"Yes," Lance was saying, "what would the entire package cost, approximately?"

There was a motion to postpone the adoption of the security system. This motion carried.

"We're not forgetting about it." Lance patted Jerry's arm, then shook hands with the salesman. "It's just, well, premature to consider it this year. As Lida pointed out"—he turned to smile at her—"there are so many other worthy projects that the committee ought to be spending its money on."

Jerry caught her arm as she left the room. "You sure know how to hurt a guy, don't you?" he said.

35

Duvivier remembered Carol Bradley's progress at the publishing house of Seare and Jolly. It had been marked.

When, at Jolly's urging, she had bid her young stockbroker friend good-bye, she traded her cubicle for an office, a real office. And then, a bigger office.

And when Mrs. Jolly decided to spend the holidays in Noroton, Carol Bradley's L-shaped metal desk was replaced with a peachwood table. It had no drawers. And a typewriter would have affronted its glossy veneer, its long, slender legs.

Now Carol Bradley had a secretary—or, rather, an assistant. Mrs. Jolly had decided to stay in the Noroton house the year round.

The assistant consented to let Duvivier stand in the Bradley doorway and tilt inside. But he hovered in the vicinity of Duvivier's shoulder, just in case.

"Carol," Duvivier said, "I've orchestrated a little something. A joke. You're involved in it."

"Hiya, Jack!" Carol pushed her glasses onto the top of her head and leaned back into her chair.

The assistant relaxed, resuming his seat and his magazine.

"I met a woman," Duvivier continued. "Her name is Lida—"

"Oh," she interrupted, "the vermouth and lemon. So that *was* you."

"She called?"

"Yup. We thought she was crazy. But then we figured that it had to be you."

"You've sent her the book?"

"We called the warehouse. They're sending it."

"Thank you." He heard the telephone buzz behind him and heard the assistant murmur into it.

"Himself," the janizary announced.

Carol Bradley lifted the receiver but covered the mouthpiece. "Don't mention it," she said. "And, Jack?" She winked. "Would you close that door on your way out?"

Duvivier closed the door. He would walk, he thought. He needed to walk.

He had not been wrong about needing that scene. And damn! Thus far he'd managed only the opening line: "I just love your murders," his victim would say, her blue-black hair falling prettily across her face.

Yes, he would walk. And as he walked he would decide how, when, and where Lida was to die.

36

Jackson R.W. Bishop stood outside the New York Public Library and pondered murder. He had never planned a murder before. It would be a new sensation.

There was Christine Rivers, certainly, but that couldn't be called murder. Assault, perhaps, with cause. But without intent to kill.

He remembered her face in the lamplight, the nose akilter, the blood welling in her throat. His breath came in little gasps and he leaned against the building.

"You okay, mister?" A little boy stared up at him, his lips pursed, his eyes troubled.

"Don't talk to anyone!" A woman yanked at the boy's arm, pulling him off his feet.

"I'm okay," he called after the child.

He sighed, his breathing pattern normal now. Jack's death

had been timely, but none of his doing. He hadn't even seen Jack's body, or what was left of it. Still, he felt that Jack, somehow, had died in his behalf.

Jackson R.W. Bishop imagined Lida, a knife jutting from her abdomen. "Don't be silly," she would holler, pulling it out, flinging it across the room. Or with her head enveloped in a plastic bag. "Stop," she would say, fighting free. "This isn't funny."

How would he kill her?

He could shoot her, but he hadn't a pistol. Poison? She would never notice. She had eaten two helpings of those hideous hash-browns in the Howard Johnson's.

He could arrange to meet her in some crime-ridden part of Washington. A place where she would be murdered and possibly raped beforehand. Or, depending on the neighborhood, afterward. He saw a gang of thugs backing away. "Get fucked," she was screaming at them, "I'm waiting for someone."

He laughed out loud. Lida did, on the face of it, seem invincible. His laughter was drawing attention from passersby.

Still. He cautioned himself sufficiently to halt his merriment with the thought of what she knew. Lida's death was no trifle.

But what was at the root of the trouble he was having? Why wouldn't Lida stay dead? She was infuriating. He thought and thought.

And then he knew. Jackson R.W. Bishop was at the root of it, the wrong man for the job.

Duvivier had a flair for violence that quite eluded Bishop. Duvivier could set a man, asshole-first, onto a spike and laugh into the darkness. Or fuck a woman with grotesque implements until she bled to death. Duvivier could slash a man's stomach and watch the viscera slither to the floor. And then he would describe the mess.

It was Duvivier who must consider the exasperating Lida's

141

death, but later. Jackson R.W. Bishop meanwhile would go inside and check out this pseudonym business.

゜Ｃ

He got off the elevator on the third floor, with Room 315 his destination. He had once seen a book dedicated to Room 315 of the New York Public Library. He could not remember which book it was and, after some seconds, gave it up. What did it matter?

Once there, he was immediately distressed by the enormity of the card catalog. So many drawers. And so many people using them.

He walked to the D drawers and looked down the row. He found the one that would contain Duvivier. He began sifting through the cards, without removing the drawer. Someone behind him gave a long-suffering sigh. He turned, nodded an apology, and took the drawer to a table.

Only two of Duvivier's books were listed. That rather angered him. He wondered about the rest. Then he saw a notice that referred him to a newer catalog. This turned out to be a row of blue books on a shelf in yet another part of the room.

He was partially appeased. All of Duvivier's books were listed here, but none of the entries bore any author's name but that one. He walked to the information counter and asked how he might find the real name of an author using a pseudonym.

"What's the name?" the clerk asked.

"Duvivier," he said, expecting that he would have to spell it.

"Oh, yes!" The clerk brightened. "That's pretty recent. Let's see." He stood rubbing his nose, his eyes panning the room. "Try bookcase number four, over there. Down at the bottom. It should be in *Current Biography*. They're indexed." The clerk immediately turned his attention to the person who stood behind Duvivier.

He stooped and read the indices of several of the volumes.

Up to 1974. He could not find 1975. But it was, he knew, a stupid search. Worthless. He glanced up from the spot where he crouched and saw a woman reading from the 1975 volume. The hell with it.

He moved into another room, one with long tables and rows of incandescent lamps. He stood near the door, wondering whether to go back into the street or stay here awhile.

"Help you?" A crisp accent. British.

He found a buxom woman with very red lipstick smiling up at him. "I don't suppose," he said halfheartedly, "there's any way of getting the real name of an author using a pseudonym."

"Oh, yes," she said, "there are several books you can look at." She turned to a small boxed catalog just behind her desk. "P-s-e-u . . ." flipping the cards very quickly.

He read over her shoulder.

Her fingers stopped. "PSEUDONYMS," the card read, "SEE ANONYMS AND PSEUDONYMS." She closed the drawer with a hint of embarrassment and opened another. "Here we are," she announced, stepping aside. "Look through these and then go on to Section Seventy-four, over there." She gestured toward the far wall.

He thanked her and listened to her heels click out of range.

None of the books in Section Seventy-four contained any of his names. Most of the volumes were not contemporary, but dealt with authors long dead. They seemed exercises, largely, the tedious sort of work for which doctoral degrees were awarded. The one entry in the small card file which had seemed promising—a book by someone named Gribbons—was not on the shelf.

How had Lida found the Wendolyn name? She had told him. Yes. At the Library of Congress. He would have to try there. He would do it soon.

He was eager to leave New York. He was tired of it, tired of people asking at the end of every sentence if he knew what they meant.

Outside, the snow was fast turning to slush. New York, he thought, was very like Madrid. The buildings here were taller, of course. And there were fewer trees. But the weather was the same and the people were the same. The great cities of the world, he decided, were all alike.

❧

He slipped into the bookstore, largely to escape the wind. He purchased a notepad and, as it was being rung up, read the placard affixed to the register.

Ah! *The Play of Herod*, the sign said, would be performed tomorrow night. And, he noted with relief, by former members of the New York Pro Musica. Where? Washington National Cathedral, Washington D.C. It would be ably done, then.

He remembered the campus production that someone had arranged many years ago. The innocents, young boys from the town, perhaps eight or nine years old, stood center stage awaiting the wrath of the evil king. One of them, an Oriental lad, yawned profusely. Another, a young Billy Budd, all pallor and platinum, had to drop his head to hide his laughter. Even dead, the boy kept breaking up, his thin shoulders heaving under his white robe. The others fought hard to ignore him.

The narrator, a sophomore whose name he could not recall, had stuttered over the fine MacLeish text. And the voices! They seemed to have been chosen from random shower stalls in the various college dormitories.

Afterward, he had eavesdropped on members of the audience. Paul Riley had wondered if the singer who had joined in Rachel's lamentation—the one in woman's garb—was indeed the man who had played the shepherd at the start of the play. His students had wondered how the archangel had managed to stand so still throughout the production.

Oh, academe! He had never regretted leaving it behind.

❦

In the lobby of his New York hotel, Duvivier watched the people pass. Occasionally he would pause to write.

The characters—victim and killer—had been fixed. But where? And how?

He pocketed the pen and watched the lobby traffic again.

A hotel—even a landmark like the Watergate—wouldn't do. He needed to take advantage of the setting, and not in any obvious way. That meant that the White House, the Capitol, and the various monuments and memorials were out.

But what about the Supreme Court? That hadn't been done. The place had a nice, sepulchral air. And wasn't there a floating staircase in the building? He thought he'd seen photos of that. Ah, yes. He closed his eyes and visualized Lida's body lying there, pale and limp and broken. Yes, there! Her luxurious hair would be tousled, but becomingly so. And beneath that jet-black hair, bright red rivulets would flow, would stain the alabaster stair. Ah, yes!

Innocent, indestructable Lida—like the innocents in *Herod*, doomed to slaughter.

It was then that he saw the light bulb, a small, bare globule so very like the ones in comic strips. The ones that signify the dawning of an idea. How much more fitting *that* would be: *The Play of Herod*. Washington National Cathedral, Washington, D.C. It was perfect. He smiled and uncapped his pen. And Lida would love it, if she knew. Upon the pad he wrote: *Murder in the Cathedral*.

And then he walked to a row of telephones, reaching for the envelope upon which he'd written the number.

145

37

Lida measured a cup of apricot nectar into the blender. Then she held a tablespoon heaped with yogurt over it. She let the yogurt plop off the spoon into the bright yellow morass. She capped the container, then stood absentmindedly listening to the whir of the machine.

The Ronald Wendolyn treatise on Renaissance stagecraft was beside her. It lay open to the flap where his photograph appeared. Whenever she looked at it, she felt giddy. She remembered ogling a photo of the Four Lads in much the same way and with much the same effect in her early teens. "Jesus," she said out loud, "here I am, America's oldest groupie!"

He had clearly lied about his name. He could not, she reasoned, have taught under an assumed name. And there it was, in print, under the picture: Ronald Wendolyn, Assistant Professor, Murdock College, New Hampshire.

The photo had a yearbook quality. It had been taken against a pale background and cropped to just under his shoulders. His eyes focused on something to the left of the photographer, as eyes were wont to do in photos of that ilk.

His hair seemed thinner than it had last night. And this morning. His mouth was the same. A fantastic mouth.

He had a wife, he had said. Was that a lie as well? Who might she be? Someone like George Sand. Or Anaïs Nin. Shit. He did not, she decided, have a wife.

The telephone rang. Diana, probably. And about time, too. She would tell Diana, of course. But it would be like repeating a story to a newcomer in the presence of those who had already heard it. The edge of it would be dulled. Or something.

She would sharpen it.

I've been to an orgy, she would say. I slept with four men, all at once. Duvivier. Ronald Wendolyn. And somebody named Grisone. And somebody named Bishop.

But it wasn't like that. It wasn't like that at all.

She picked up the phone on the fourth ring.

It was not Diana.

"I . . ." she stammered, "I really hadn't expected . . ." And she hadn't. Hoped, sure. Expected? Never.

Lida went to her desk, pulled open the drawer, and took out the diary Diana had given her last year for Christmas. She had protested when she'd opened the package, "I'm not the type!"

But Diana had insisted that she was. "The world deserves a written record of your adventures." She'd laughed. "There probably won't even be enough space for all of them."

But there was more than enough. Lida kept it as a log rather than a diary. She confined her markings to a mere sentence or two. Sometimes, not even a sentence. A fragment. And she did it with a sense of duty rather than any real zest.

The last thing she'd written was on Monday: "Diana to NH." Well, she'd take up where that left off. She tried to reconstruct the events in their proper sequence.

Done, she put the book away, then took something else from the drawer—a tightly wadded piece of paper. She hesitated, held it in her fist. Hell, why not? She smoothed the sheet of paper against her thigh before she wrote on it. Then she replaced it, closed the drawer.

She sat there feeling stupid.

Could he, Duvivier, want her? She could not believe it.

Even Jerry Felton hadn't wanted her. None of them had wanted her, really. They had wanted the way she looked, not her at all.

She thought of the movie *Georgy Girl,* and her favorite scene. The one when Georgy comes down the staircase, ridiculously overwrought. Eye goo. Rouge spots. Feathers. And all the people in the room below stop and stare. And then James Mason goes over and takes her hand and dances with her. And the people stop staring and dance again, because even Georgy has to be all right if James Mason would dance with her after she'd come down the stairs looking that way.

Something about that scene really got to Lida. Something about being fat and frumpy and ridiculous—and wanted anyway. Accepted anyway. And by James Mason, no less.

Lida had always wanted to be less than her peacock self— wanted to be Georgy, coming down the stairs. Had always wanted to know, the way a dog like Georgy *had* to know when Mason walked across that floe of silence and took her hand: Georgy, you're ace-high with me. Ace-high, no matter what you look like, no matter what you say.

Jesus.

And now Duvivier was there, playing Mason. Duvivier, to

whom even she must seem so very ordinary, so very Georgy, Duvivier, worldwide womanizer, who wanted *her*.

But God, she had to get out of here. Had to get out of here so he couldn't call back and change his mind.

38

Diana walked into the shambles that was Lida's living room and called her name. There was no reply. She hadn't expected one. Lida's car was gone, and she hadn't been there to answer her phone.

A week's wardrobe, at least, was heaped on the living-room chair. Two pair of pantyhose lay rumpled at the foot of the stairs. Another pair hung wanly over the side of a wicker wastebasket.

She remembered the wrath Lida had directed against pantyhose manufacturers. "You know why the damned things never fit?" she had shouted. "You know why? Because the assholes sit around the planning table and can't bring themselves to use the word 'crotch,' that's why."

She went into Lida's bedroom. And then, of course, she thought of Lou.

She glanced around the room. She could not imagine bringing Lou, or bringing anyone, here.

It looked as though it served as the dressing compartment for an entire chorus line. More pantyhose. Creams and perfumes and eye makeup. Shoes and boots strewn about. It was amazing that Lida appeared out of this rubble, daily, like a phoenix from the ashes.

Diana admired the clothes that Lida wore, and more, the way she wore them. Carelessly. As though they couldn't help but look good.

She had said something of the sort to Lida once, and Lida had laughed, lapsing into the black dialect that made Diana cringe. "Oh, yes, my *fine* self. I like to dress my *fine* self in this *fine* way . . ." There had been two black students in the room at the time, and they had laughed.

Lou had called last night while Diana was in her bedroom being "sick." At least, she thought it had been Lou.

"That guy called" was the way Eddie had phrased it.

Could it have been Allen?

No. Then Eddie would have said, "Some guy called." *That* guy meant Lou, whose voice each of her children had heard.

She wished it had been Allen.

She looked at the clock. She decided she would wait for half an hour, and then, if Lida hadn't come, she would leave a note. She took a stack of fashion magazines off the chair, put them on the floor, and settled into the seat. She would need something to read. Something to look at. Something to keep from thinking.

She picked up *L'Officiel* and leafed through it. No. No. No. No. None of these clothes would suit her. They were all for someone younger. Or for someone more daring. For someone like Lida.

She remembered a woman she had seen in the street. From behind, the woman had seemed a girl. The swing of her hips. The length of her hair. And then Diana had passed her, glancing back. She was embarrassed to be looking at someone dressed so foolishly. She had resolved that she would never dress that way.

But why was she thinking about clothes? Lida's influence again. But she hadn't gone too far. She would not, as Lida sometimes did, spend whole weekends surrounded by hand-washables, spread like scarecrows to dry. She'd gone just far enough.

She would not adorn herself as though she were entering some contest.

She put the magazine aside and prowled the room for more substantial reading. A book. She reached for the one on Lida's night table. And her hand stopped dead.

It was Ronald Wendolyn's book. *Renaissance Stagecraft.* Dear God, why did Lida have it? Did Lida already know about Allen, about New Hampshire? Had Lida arranged it? Was she going to spring from the closet, laughing, "Aha! Holding out on me, Diana!" She waited, but Lida didn't appear.

It was a curious coincidence. That was all.

She picked it up, flipped through its pages. She found the photograph. So that was the man who had lived in Allen's house. The man who had endowed the Wendolyn Professorship. The man who . . .

Strange.

She looked at the clock again. More than half an hour had elapsed. She would leave Lida a note and get home in time to make supper for the boys.

She went to Lida's desk. She pulled open the drawer, looking for paper. She smiled.

There was Lida's list. The tally she had drawn up of all the men she'd slept with. It had been crumpled, she noticed, and then smoothed out again. She thought of Lida's anguish over

Jerry and unfolded it, pressing it open with the side of her hand. It was a good sign, probably, that Lida hadn't thrown it away.

She looked at the last name.

But the last name wasn't Jerry's. The last name was Duvivier. And then a line had been drawn through that name, and the name Ronald Wendolyn printed alongside.

Impossible. Ronald Wendolyn was dead. Allen had said so. Diana could close her eyes and hear Allen's voice saying so. "Very dead."

She folded the list, feeling crazy. It was all a joke, wasn't it? It was some sinister joke that Lida was playing. It was Lida's way of getting even with her for cutting short last night's conversation. Or Allen's way of laughing at her. Lida and Allen's way of laughing at her.

She took the list up again, looking for Allen's name. Not there. God, she *was* crazy. She put the list in her purse.

She called her children. No answer.

She called the college. The secretary was just leaving, she said. But yes, Lida had called. Lida was ill, didn't Diana know? She had canceled all her classes tomorrow. Flu or something. You're welcome.

Flu? Lida never had flu. She never took the flu shots that the college offered and she never got the flu. Diana saw the diary then and opened it without any of her customary soul-searching.

Monday's entry in felt-tip pen: "Diana to NH."

Then, in another ink: "Duvivier! In person! In bed! Blitzed Bill. Diana blitzed me. Blitzed J and was Sempled. Just did call S&J. And Duvivier (wonderful liar!) is Ronald Wendolyn (can't deny it, picture and all)! He (not he, but He) comes tomorrow. All this and Herod too."

Diana puzzled over this entry. *Had* Lida met Duvivier?

153

Surely she would have known if Lida had. She read the thing again. If Lida had met Duvivier while she, Diana, was in New Hampshire, she could not have known. Such was obviously the case.

What had Lida done to Bill? No time to wonder. J must be Jerry. She couldn't fathom S&J. Nor Herod. But the fact that Duvivier was Ronald Wendolyn—what else could that entry mean?—made her shudder. Because Ronald Wendolyn was a murderer. And Ronald Wendolyn was dead.

She picked up the telephone and asked for the New Hampshire area code.

39

Lida drove, keeping the engine at red-line much of the way. Occasionally she would squint at the speedometer, then lighten her foot on the gas. But her caution would never last.

She was on the Baltimore-Washington Parkway, heading into town. Lord knows, the cops were always waiting for her here. If they stopped her again, she decided, she would leap from the car, screaming over her shoulder, "You'll never take me alive, copper!" And then go live deep in the hills, the Blue Ridge, maybe, and never drive again.

She would call the Department of Motor Vehicles tomorrow or the day after. Tell them she was sorry that she'd missed their date. But she'd been in the hospital. For open-heart surgery. Daws had been pecking at it.

The light was red at North Capitol Street. She switched the radio on. Jimi Hendrix, asking if she had ever been to Electric Ladyland. The tail end of the song, where the voices wind down, exhorting the listener to make love.

She turned the volume so high that a pedestrian turned to look at her, though the roof was up and her windows were rolled shut.

Despite her tenure at Brady State College she couldn't unravel all of Hendrix's words. She liked, though, what she thought she heard, liked the angel imagery, liked the way the words seemed to glimmer as they were sung. Good and evil. Electric love.

She shouldn't let herself in for this. She should stand him up. Not give him a chance to fuck her over. She *wouldn't* let herself in for this.

It was then that Lida saw the parking space on Connecticut Avenue. She backed into it with flair.

She ordered spaghetti alla carbonara. That shouldn't conflict with the nectar and yogurt too much. And she wouldn't have dessert, because then she might break out tomorrow. God. She didn't want to see him with a pimple in the middle of her forehead. Well, what the hell. She'd *see* him. What was the point of standing him up. Besides . . . She held her fork in midair, remembering.

"Everything all right?" the waitress asked.

"Delicious," Lida said. "The best ever."

40

Diana sat in Lida's chair, the list on her lap, the phone laid over it, receiver pressed tight against her ear. She waited for the atonal intrigue of chimes and beeps and circuit static to end, the transferring to begin, humans taking up where machinery left off. The Murdoch College switchboard differed from its counterpart at Brady State only in the substitution of a twang for semi-Southern slur.

Finally, an abrupt announcement was made: "Riley."

Diana hesitated. She'd met Riley. Good manners dictated that she acknowledge him. But, "I'm calling Professor Dilworth," she said, mustering a voice that Lida would have called "prissy," a voice that might have suited Jane Austen herself, a voice that defended against men like Paul Riley.

"Sure, babe," he replied. "He's on this extension. I'll just go down the hall and get him."

The phone dropped with rude clatter onto Riley's desktop.

Diana heard him trudge away, the way he'd trudged away at the luncheon. She sat tapping her finger against the dial.

An extension was lifted and Diana heard Allen clear his throat. "This is Professor Dilworth," he said.

"Allen"—she was talking too loud—"it's Diana."

"Diana! How wonderful! I was just about to call you."

"Allen, listen," she said, "I want to talk to you about Wendolyn. About the . . ." She stopped just short of "murder."

"Wendolyn? Come on, just say you want to talk to me. God knows, I want to talk to you." He seemed amused. He thought it a ruse, a woman's trick.

"Allen," she said, "please."

He laughed. "All right. Of course we'll talk—but in person. That's why I was about to call."

"About Wendolyn?" her voice went shrill.

"I was calling to say that I'm coming down there tomorrow, and that I'd like to see you."

"Are you sure he's dead, Allen, are you?"

He sounded wary. "Wendolyn? Of course. What's wrong? Tell me what it is."

Diana made no reply.

"Won't you tell me?" A cajoling voice. As though he were talking to someone on a ledge. Someone about to jump.

There was a lull, filled with the shuffle of Riley reentering his own office. They both waited, but the line remained open. Diana took a deep breath. It was then that the phone was replaced in its cradle.

"I know I sound crazy," she said. "Maybe I am. I don't know where to start. But, look, you needn't come down. That seems, well, excessive."

"Nonsense. The college is paying my way. I wasn't sure they'd go for it, because it is stretching it a bit. But I've managed to talk them into sending me down for research purposes."

Research. Travel vouchers. It was all so sane. So reassuringly sane. It calmed her. "Where?" she asked. "At the Library of Congress?"

"A lot more lively than that. Some former members of the New York Pro Musica are giving a performance of *The Play of Herod* down there. It isn't performed very often, and—"

"Herod," she shouted, "as in *King* Herod?"

"Diana, what is the matter with you?" He listened. "You aren't crying, are you? Has something happened?"

"I don't know," she said. "Something might."

"I have my flight number and all that right here somewhere. Just a moment."

She heard papers riffling. Then he was back. She blurted into the phone before he could speak, "Allen, he's alive. Wendolyn is alive."

A weighty pause. The connection grew hollow, suddenly, appropriately. "How do you know?" he asked.

Diana did cry then, but quietly, so that he couldn't tell. "It's a friend of mine. You know, I told you about her. Lida. The one who—"

"Yes, I remember. But what—?"

"Allen, I'm so afraid he'll murder her, too."

"But how? Why?"

She worked very hard at her voice. "I'll explain when you get here," she said. "I'll tell you all of it."

"I hope so."

"Shall I meet your plane?"

"Flight 739 from Boston," he said. "It arrives at four-thirty-two in the afternoon at, let me see, Baltimore-Washington International. Is that handy to you?"

"Yes. I'll be there."

"Diana. Under the circumstances. That is, *even* under the circumstances, it will be good to see you."

"Yes," she said, remembering, warming. "Oh, yes."

41

Christ, he'd probably die with an erection. Felt the way he had at fifteen, on the bus, his books clapped over his crotch so no one could see.

Funny, how it would happen. And this time, all it took was the word. One word. Murder.

42

A hoodlum loitered on the corner near Lida's car. He watched her approach it.

Lida watched back. What was his problem? If he thought he was going to snatch her purse, he'd better think again.

Maybe he would try to rape her. Ha! She'd let him get his pants down, she decided, and then she'd point at his pecker and laugh and laugh and laugh. And then she'd bring her heel down on his instep, jam her ignition key up his nose, and knee him in the balls. Then . . .

He didn't move toward her. He just watched. Expectantly. And with, yes, amusement.

Had he done something to her car?

She turned the key. The engine gave its customary eager growl. And then she put the car in gear.

Something *was* wrong. She checked the emergency brake.

No, it was off. She hit the gas pedal again, more determinedly than before.

The car started forward. Then there was a loud crunch. Then the car rocked back and stalled.

That fucker! And here he was, now, coming toward her.

She took the keys out of the ignition, ready to gouge.

He knocked at her window, holding a little placard.

Lida cranked the window open and snatched it.

"NOTICE!" it began. Oh, no. She jumped out of the car to the accompaniment of his simian hoots and hollers.

"Nothing personal," he assured her, barely able to get the words out, he was laughing so hard.

"Get out of here," she said, "or I'll jam these keys up your nose."

That amused him even more.

Lida looked at her car, which was trussed and bound. The Iron Maiden, the Denver Boot, the Yellow Submarine. Whatever you chose to call it, it was the sunny little clamp that the District of Columbia police affix to the front wheel of the vehicles on their shit list.

Lida's attempt to drive away had bent the thing a bit. But it had held. The hoodlum, however, had pointed to a passage on the card. So now the police were going to fine her for damaging city property as well. It was a racket. They got you coming and going. They'd probably ticket her in the morning, too, for being in the parking space longer than the allotted two hours.

She stalked away. Let them have the goddamned car. Let them sell it at auction. Let them shove it up their ass.

She wished she'd had dessert, after all.

She could call Diana. But, no. That was too much to ask, her driving all the way downtown. She could take a bus. But she hated buses. She could take a cab. Yes. She would take a cab. She walked and walked in search of one, clear to Dupont Circle. None in sight. She peered down a side street and saw the Embassy Row Hotel. That's what she would do. Stay downtown.

She backtracked to the People's Drugstore on the Circle and bought what she would need. A toothbrush. A razor. Nail polish. A new pair of pantyhose. That way, she wouldn't have to wash out the pair she was wearing.

The Embassy Row Hotel, she remembered, once ran a radio commercial wherein the hotel purported to speak. "I am the Embassy Row Hotel," it would say, just before Lida would switch to another station. She went through the entrance feeling as though she had walked through a great glass mouth.

There were three women behind the desk, jabbering. One broke away to attend to Lida, but the others continued their talk.

" . . . and he snores like this, half the night." The woman rattled her tongue against the roof of her mouth, producing a loud trill.

"You ought to hear *mine* grind his teeth," the other countered.

Lida thought of Mrs. Semple. And then, inexplicably, of Diana. She really ought to call Diana. Just in case. In case? She wondered at the phrase.

"Who is this?" Lida said into the receiver. "Timmy?"

"Eddie."

"Put your mother on," she said.

"She's not here."

"What do you mean, not there? Where is she?"

"I dunno."

"Well, *ask*, you moron. Ask your brothers."

"They aren't here."

"Well, tell her I called," Lida said.

"I can't," he answered, "I'm goin' out."

"Well, leave a note. You can write, can't you?"

If Diana wasn't with her kids, where would she be? Probably with what's-his-face. The one who comes for coffee. Christ, if that's all he did after all this time, he must be queer. And not only queer. He probably snored. And ground his teeth. Poor Diana. Her ovaries had probably turned to powder by now. What Diana needed was someone like Duvivier.

She leaned back, remembering the whole thing. His silly questions. The way he had pressed his face against her leg and then withdrawn, startled by the stubble.

She grabbed her handbag and dumped its contents on the bed. She found the razor and ripped the cardboard free. And then she changed her mind. No. She would go to the Elizabeth Arden salon tomorrow. Have a half-leg. And what they euphemistically called a bikini. And, if they could squeeze her in, she'd have a paraffin bath, and a massage.

Georgy Girl, coming down the stairs, sleek and paraffined.

She wished she'd said that to the departmental secretary: I won't be meeting my classes tomorrow. I'm going to have a paraffin bath. Yes, at Elizabeth Arden. That would have been so much better than flu. Flu was so ordinary. And they'd have loved it. She was the only person in the English Department who could have gotten away with saying it. Maybe the only person in the whole school. A paraffin bath.

She looked at the rubble she had created, glad to have broken the noncommittal cleanliness of the room. Her history—her recent history, anyway—was there in that heap. The theater stubs. The soiled hankies. The matchbooks from restaurants about town. God, there was even a tube of spermicidal jelly.

One by one she hurled these things at the wastebasket, missing more often than not. But she didn't throw the jelly away. She would give that to Diana. "Here," she would say, "for your hope chest."

She wished she'd brought the Wendolyn book along. She'd begun it at the Library Committee meeting, before she'd discovered that the jacket bore his photograph. She could have finished it tonight. She took up a novel she'd found in her purse. Nabokov. Close, she thought, but no cigar.

She read until she fell asleep.

Lida dreamed she was at Diana's, standing in front of the refrigerator. "I have a taste for something," she announced, though she was alone there, "but I don't know what it is." She opened the refrigerator door and hung on it, scanning the shelves.

There were men inside, everywhere. They were in the egg bins and the butter keeper. They were peering around milk cartons and juice cans. One was leaning against some half-and-half, as though waiting for someone, killing time.

Charles was one of the men. He was wrapped in cellophane, a neat little collar tied around the bag to keep him fresh. "No," Lida said, "that's not what I want."

The psychiatrist was in the freezer sitting on some breasts and thighs. Chicken breasts and thighs, of course. "Lord, no," Lida said, slamming the freezer shut.

The hoodlum emerged from a foil-capped bowl, exposing himself. Lida pointed at his penis and laughed and laughed and laughed.

Jerry was on the glass shelf at the bottom, treading water in a half-filled jar of artichoke hearts. They were banging against his shoulder and he had to keep pushing them away to keep

165

his head above the brine. "Uh-uh," Lida said.

What was it she wanted? She closed the refrigerator and moved to one of the cupboards above the stove. The one where Diana kept crackers and pretzels and chips. She had just reached up, about to settle for something, when Duvivier, life-size, appeared and caught her hand.

"Let's go on a diet," he said. "Lock ourselves in a room and eat only each other."

She woke up smiling.

43

"Don't you see"—Allen strained to keep the exasperation from his voice—"if he *is* alive, you'll know him. You'll remember him. I've never met the man."

"Dilworth," Riley said, "this whole thing is a crock. And what's your girlfriend going to say when I show up, huh?" The word "girlfriend" came out pinched when he said it. He gave Wendolyn's name, when he spoke it, the same inflection.

"Diana knows something," Allen said.

Riley narrowed his eyes.

"I don't know what it is," Allen continued, "or how it ties in, but she knows something."

"The college won't pay for it," Riley said. "It's way out of my area."

"I'll pay for it," Allen said.

Riley's lips parted. His teeth were revealed. "Sheesh!" he said.

167

44

Duvivier settled into a window seat and took a magazine to ward away potential chatter. He needn't have. The gentleman on his right carried a similar shield, a weathered copy of *The Wall Street Journal*. It would be a good flight.

He had lied to Lida again, saying that he would arrive in Washington late that afternoon. In fact, he would arrive late that morning. But such a small lie, a lie that would give him a few hours at the Library of Congress.

And then a few hours with her.

And then . . . *The Play of Herod*.

He had rather shocked himself by suggesting that she come to his hotel. Sporting with the doomed Lida seemed heartless, even for Duvivier. Why had he done that? She would have been willing to meet him there, at the cathedral. That, it seemed, had been his plot, even as he dialed her number.

Had she asked for those hours? He remembered their talk.

No. The revision had been his own doing.

Though threatened by her in the abstract—by what she knew and what she might learn—he was aware of an absence of strain in her presence. He had, for instance, mentioned his days as a teacher. That was in response to something she had said of her own teaching experience. It was a harmless enough remark. And he had mentioned Riley. But only that the man lumbered around the campus with his pants always stuck in the crack of his ass. And Lida had laughed, saying that she knew the type.

But the fact that he had dropped his guard, or very nearly dropped it, only served to convince him of the danger she posed. No question, Lida must die.

"I just want to relax." That's what she told him, early on. Not a notable line, but a notable feeling. And yet her honesty, if that's what it was, seemed more habit than moral code.

He smiled, recalling the attempts he had made to anger her, to send her away. Six pigs and a gazelle. Or had it been the other way around? Yes, it was six gazelles and a pig. If anything, he had confirmed the very persistence he now feared. Oh, the pity of it!

He remembered holding her in the predawn gloom. "Tell me how you feel," he had said, "in words, tell me."

"I don't feel in words," she had replied, her voice muffled by the proximity of her body to his own. She told him, then, with those fingers.

He laid the magazine across his lap.

Perhaps Duvivier was not heartless. Perhaps he was generous.

45

Lida walked along Connecticut Avenue, straining to see if her car was still padlocked in place in front of the restaurant. But when she reached the Elizabeth Arden salon, she was still too far away to tell.

She pulled at the solid red door. Then she saw the little brass plaque directing her to push. A woman behind her gave a "tsk" and tapped her foot impatiently. Lida looked down at the foot, at the little black pump with the initials, back to back, on the leather: Givenchy. "Tsk," Lida returned, pushing open the door and then not bothering to hold it.

She took the elevator to the third floor. The wrinkled black man at the controls nodded at her, as though she were a regular. In fact, Lida had been here only once before and had been sent away in ignominy, dismissed as not hairy enough for the waxing procedure to be performed.

She walked to the reception desk. "Half-leg and bikini," she said with authority.

The woman behind the desk gave her a once-over. "You haven't shaved?" she questioned, her eyelids at half-mast.

"Nope," Lida answered.

"For at least four weeks? Are you certain?"

"I've been in a funk," Lida said, "so I haven't, honest."

"I think Danielle is free."

The woman in the Givenchy shoes reappeared. She was Danielle.

℃

"How are you today?" Danielle asked, leading Lida into the pastel privacy of one of the narrow rooms along the corridor.

"Very hairy," Lida said, disrobing warily while Danielle clanked and puttered with some utensils. When Lida was naked, Danielle handed her a pink kimono and gestured at a table. It was very much like a gynecologist's table, but without the stirrups.

"I have a few hairs on my nipples," Lida said, eyeing the vat of hot wax and attempting, therefore, to be friendly.

"We don't do nipples," Danielle said, pulling the robe aside and arranging Lida's leg on the table. She rolled a tiny pink towel and placed it over Lida's vulva. "Hold this," she said.

Lida raised herself on her fists and watched Danielle spoon the hot wax along her groin. "Is this going to hurt?" Lida asked, wishing she had held the door.

Danielle patted ice chips over the wax and tapped at it. She looked at Lida and smiled for the first time. "Yes," she said. The smile broadened when she pried up a corner of the hardened patch. "Lean back," she directed, "and take a deep breath."

And then she yanked. It was like a thousand Band-Aids being pulled off all at once. A thousand Band-Aids taped where none had ever been taped before. It took the hair out to the roots.

"Skip the other side," Lida said, sitting hurriedly, "and skip the legs."

Danielle poured some pink lotion onto a wad of cotton. "Come on, now," she said, "this will make it feel better."

"What is it? Hydrochloric acid?"

"It's a soothing lotion." She motioned Lida back onto the table. She arranged her leg again. And then she patted the lotion on.

"It *does* feel better," Lida said.

"Of course." Danielle walked back and took up the spoon.

"Wait a minute." Lida sat up and looked down at herself. Her dark isosceles triangle of pubic hair had gone scalene. "I look silly with only one side done, don't I?" she asked, hoping Danielle would soften and tell her, no, it was the *in* thing this year to look like King Kong on the left side and a ballerina on the right.

Danielle didn't reply. She stood, stirring the thick brown wax. Finally, transferring some from the caldron to a small aluminum pot, she spoke to Lida. "Well," she said, "is he worth it?"

"So far." Lida sighed, reclining again. But she still had the rest of the bikini and two half-legs to go.

Lida wondered if her Blue Cross policy would cover this. The way she felt, it ought to. And did she have to tip Danielle for this? Obviously she did. Danielle stood and waited. "What now?" Lida groaned.

"Your underarms," Danielle said.

"Oh, shit." Lida raised her arms, exposing the pits. In true surrender, she thought.

"Still worth it, huh?" Danielle said, spooning.

And finally it was over. Danielle was gathering up her equipment, arranging it on a tray. "Next time," Danielle said, "make a forty-five-minute appointment. Then we can do something about"—she propped the door open with her well-shod foot, preparing to slip into the hall—"your little mustache."

The door whooshed closed behind her.

ꙮ

Lida handed the receptionist a nickel. "This is for Danielle," she said.

ꙮ

They were probably over Philadelphia by now, although he couldn't see the ground because of the cloud cover. He reached up to ring the little bell over his head, and the stewardess approached, smiling.

"Can I get you something, sir?" she asked.

"You can get me a bourbon. And a Washington newspaper. You have a Washington newspaper?" He looked at her breasts and then back at her face.

"Yes, sir," she said, the smile still very much in place.

What would it take, he wondered, to knock that smile off her face?

46

Jackson R.W. Bishop found himself staring at a gum-chewing person with bangs, the third such to whom he had spoken regarding Duvivier's pseudonym. He stood at the circular desk in the rotunda that served as the main reading room of the Library of Congress and gazed up toward the skylight. He wished that the statue of Justice, some one hundred feet above, would come alive, tear the blindfold from her eyes, and heave her scales down upon the mindless girl. "Thank you," he said, "for your trouble."

He walked back toward the tables that circled the room, found an empty one, and sat to consider what his next move might be, if, indeed, he bothered to make any at all.

One of the clerks wobbled up the row, dispensing books to the patrons who had ordered them. He placed a volume on Duvivier's desk and moved on.

Duvivier let his hand fall on the spine of the book. Perhaps it was a quirk of fate. Perhaps the person who had filled out the call slip listing this desk number had, inadvertently, given him the answer he sought. He looked at the title page: the 1948 volume of *The Livestock and Sanitation Journal.*

"Excuse me," someone said, "but this is *my* desk."

"And your book," Duvivier said, giving her a quick appraisal, "obviously."

They smiled at each other and he relinquished the chair.

❦

What had Lida said? What, exactly, had Lida said?

That she'd compiled the bibliography required of all English graduate students here. "Measured out my life in index cards" was how she'd put it. And that she'd vowed, once her degree had been awarded, never to pass through the library portals again. "Like shopping at Klein's. It's something you want to put behind you." Yes, she'd said that. She must have written, then. Or called.

He went to a pay phone in the basement and thumbed through the heavy directory, balancing it, in part, on his upraised knee and, in part, on the narrow shelf that the telephone company provided. He dialed the number that the directory had listed and gave his request to the operator.

She smacked her lips and then told him to dial another number. That of Telephone Inquiry.

"Can't you transfer my call?"

Yes, she could. And did. Another female voice came on the line. He repeated his question and was made to wait in the vacuum called Hold. "Duvivier," the woman said when she returned. "That's the only reference I have."

"Just a moment," he stalled. "I wonder if you could tell me where you get your information."

"Where I get it?"

"Yes. How do you go about looking it up?"

175

"Oh." She laughed. "I ask Mr. Morganthaler. He looks it up."

"Could I speak to Mr. Morganthaler?" he asked.

"No, I'm sorry, he's on another line."

"I'd be glad to wait."

"Well . . . " She considered. "What is this in reference to?"

He sighed. "It's in reference to the way in which one goes about looking up the actual name of someone using a pseudonym." He wished the words were bullets, each wounding her grossly. He rather doubted that Lida would have had the patience for any of this. But obviously she had. He should be immensely flattered. He was, as a matter of fact. He picked up a section of newspaper that lay on the floor of the phone booth and looked at it. "You see," he told the woman, "I'm from *The Washington Post* and I'm doing a story on the library." He gave her the name of the first by-line that struck his eye.

"Oh, wow!" she said. "I'll get Mr. Morganthaler right away!" The phone at her end clattered onto the desk or the floor, Hold forgotten in her excitement.

"I've always felt there was a story here. A damned good story. It's about time you people got around to it." Morganthaler himself.

"Yes, well, could I come around," Duvivier said, "in half an hour, let's say? To interview you, of course."

"That's cutting it kind of close," Morganthaler said. "This place here isn't exactly . . . you see, we never see anyone here. We deal with people over the phone. You might say we never see the light of day." He chuckled. "You can put that in your article. Never see the light of day."

"When shall I come?"

"Oh, why don't you come at three or thereabouts. The girls will be on their break. It'll give me a chance to kind of clear

176

things up a bit." He told Duvivier, in elaborate detail, how he would find his way to the Telephone Inquiry section.

"Is your story on the library as a whole," Morganthaler asked, "or just on pseudonyms? Jennie said it was pseudonyms."

"Actually," he replied, "it's on the Telephone Inquiry section."

"No kidding!" The man's cheeks swelled and his left eyebrow twitched. "Does that mean they'll be taking pictures?" He looked over Duvivier's shoulder, as though he'd somehow overlooked the presence of the photographer and would now rectify that rude act.

"The photographer will be along in a day or two. We do it that way so that you can plan to wear something becoming."

Morganthaler clasped his hands together, saying, "Well, anything I can do to help you. Anything at all."

The books came to the Cataloging Section from the Copyright Division. The information on pseudonyms—those too recent to be recorded in the 1972 Scarecrow something-or-other—was transferred from Copyright to Cataloging to Telephone Inquiry. It was simple. And was he going too fast?

"How do you know"—Duvivier looked up from his pad—"when an author is using a pseudonym?"

"Oh, you don't, not always. A few slip by, like that fellow who was mixed up in the Watergate business, the one who wrote all those spy novels? Now, *you* should know his name."

Duvivier didn't know, but was spared.

"Howard Hunt! That fellow. He wrote under a whole bunch

177

of names, and we never had it in our files. You see, if the author doesn't want anyone to know, the publisher won't release that information."

"Is that right!"

"Oh, yes. You take those books *The Sensuous Woman* and *The Sensuous Man?*" He missed Duvivier's lack of comprehension. "Well, right after those two came out, they came up with another one, *The Sensuous Dirty Old Man* by Mr. X? Well, I tell you, we ran around like crazy trying to find out who Mr. X was, and we couldn't. No, sir, we couldn't. But"— he winked at Duvivier—"I met the man, on business, you might say."

"You met Mr. X!" Duvivier pretended to take notes.

"Right. He's one of America's most prolific authors. You wouldn't believe it if I told you who Mr. X was."

"Who is he?" He held his pencil at the ready.

"Oh, no you don't. I know all about you reporters. No, sir. I'll take that secret to the grave."

"It must have been a terrible moral struggle," Duvivier said, "knowing and yet not being able to catalog the information."

"You bet it was. I didn't even tell my wife. But you bet it was. The library always honors the wishes of the author. Always. You might want to write that down."

Duvivier did so.

"You take that fellow you were asking about. What was his name?"

"Duvivier."

"Okay, come over here." He led him to a row of file drawers, exactly like those which housed the card catalog. "Here," he said, "you do it."

Duvivier found the name Duvivier. "There are several cards here," he said. He attempted to pull them free, but something held them. He began to examine them, one by one.

"That just means he has a lot of books. A lot of books under the name of Duvivier. Like Ellery Queen. Say, did you know that Ellery Queen is really the pseudonym of two people?"

"No!"

178

"You want to write that down? I'll keep your place."
Morganthaler inserted his fingers between the cards and gestured at the table where Duvivier had left his notepad. "Hmmph," Duvivier heard him say, "that's weird."

"What is it?"

"Somebody's written on one of these cards. So it looks like this Duvivier character might be . . . " He trailed off, oblivious of his interviewer now. Flip, flip, flip.

"What do you mean?" Duvivier thought his heart would stop. How might this have happened? He remembered the papers he'd signed, papers proffered by Carol Bradley, who at that time was, like the clerks downstairs, merely another gum-chewing person with bangs. He remembered Carol Bradley taking the wad of gum from her mouth, rolling it in her fingers, dropping it into the metal wastebasket with a thunk. And then she'd wiped the traces from her lips with one round sweeping motion of her tongue. Was that when his concentration flagged? Was that when he'd written, there on one of the forms, the name of Ronald Wendolyn?

Duvivier was imagining his hero's fingers tightening on Carol Bradley's throat, when Morganthaler interrupted.

"Pain in the you-know-what," he said, "but at least you'll get to see the kind of detective work we do around this place. We check it all out. No stone unturned, you might say." He lifted the receiver and thumbed through a worn directory.

"What is that book?" Duvivier asked.

"Just the in-house telephones," he said. "I'm trying to track Jennie down." He dialed. "Jen?" he said at last. "I've got the file card here on Duvivier. D-u-v-i-v-i-e-r." He covered the receiver and spoke to Duvivier now. "She won't remember, but it's a start."

Duvivier waited. Jennie's throat loomed, though headless, bodiless. He recalled her voice and imagined it squelched in mid-sentence. "What is this in ref—" and then a thud as she hit the floor.

"It's your handwriting," Morganthaler was saying. "That's

right. G-r-i-s-o-n-e. And the other name is Bishop, right below it."

Duvivier smiled.

Morganthaler winked. "Oh, you did. Well, Jennie, I don't care if she *was* bedridden, the fact is, you wrote on the card, one, and you didn't erase it, two, and I might have spent a whole day on this." He continued to chide her, pulling a gum eraser from his desk drawer as he spoke. He tried to reach the drawer where the cards were kept, but the cord wasn't long enough. He gestured at Duvivier to bring him the drawer. "Never, Jen," he was saying. "These cards are sacred. The Library of Congress, and don't you forget it, is the most authoritative library in the country. Yes, sir, in the country."

Duvivier laid the long thin drawer on Morganthaler's desk. He watched as Morganthaler unscrewed the button on the front of the drawer and extracted a long metal rod. He pulled the card free. "I should make you do this," he said to Jennie, "but I won't, this time. But I'll talk to you later." He hung up, wiped the eraser fragments away with his hand, and replaced the card, the rod, the drawer. "Bedridden," he muttered.

He gave Duvivier a glum look. "I'll tell you," he said, "I'd really appreciate it if you didn't put this in the story. Things like this don't happen. You see how really careful we are. Check and double-check."

"Impressive," Duvivier said.

"Still, you better not use this."

When he shook Duvivier's hand in parting, Morganthaler was hesitant. "I'd, uh, like a little insurance," he said.

"Insurance?"

"That you don't use that Duvivier thing, you know, make us look bad? I know you guys like stuff like that."

"Well, what do you have in mind?"

"After your article comes out in the paper, without any

mention of the mistake, of course, you give me a call. Okay?"

"And then?"

Morganthaler winked. His elbow jutted out like the wing of a chicken and tapped against Duvivier's side. "Mr. X," Morganthaler said. "I'll tell you who he is."

47

"Allen!" Diana rushed toward him, her arms outstretched. But just before she reached him, she lowered them to her sides. "Hello," she said almost demurely.

He stepped forward and hugged her like a bear. She became oblivious of the people that crowded past them.

"I have everything," she said, recovering, "about Wendolyn. Look." She reached into her handbag.

He put his arm around her. But Diana pulled away. She saw Paul Riley coming toward them. Her look was angry and Allen seemed to shrink before it. "Why?" it demanded.

She shook Riley's hand, lamenting that the white-glove era had passed. "Nice to see you," she said.

Allen instructed Diana to pull into the first motel she saw. She did so silently.

She was being foolish, she knew. Rude and foolish. But she could not dispel the sense of violation that Riley's presence seemed to impose. Why had Allen brought him? Would she ever get to speak to Allen alone?

She got out of the car, walking ahead of the men. She continued to lead the way in the lobby. She signed her own name in the register. "Come on," she said, still forging ahead, "come on." The clerk seemed stunned. Perhaps he envied them her eagerness.

It was only when Allen had closed the door behind them that she realized how the scene might have been read. Her face reddened. She and Allen exchanged an amused glance.

🦌

"Paul," Allen said, "I wonder if you'd mind . . ."

Riley smirked.

"Just for a moment . . ." Allen's turn to flush.

"I get you." Riley's eyes fixed on Diana. "Half an hour okay?"

🦌

"How *could* you?" Diana asked.

"He can identify Wendolyn. He *knows* him. I'm guilty, only, of taking you seriously. And, of course, of not warning you in advance that he was coming."

"Do you know what he thinks we're doing in here? *Half an hour!*" And suddenly she laughed. "Oh, he's awful!"

"I don't like him either, but at the last minute, it seemed a good idea. And if Wendolyn *is* alive, it will have been a good idea. Now, show me what you have."

"Shouldn't *he* be here?"

"All right. I'll go get him."

🦌

"She keeps a list, huh?" Riley said. "Can't wait to meet this babe."

Diana tried to take it from him. "It started as a joke," she explained. "I don't know why she kept it up."

"It's a rather lengthy list," Allen said, peering over Riley's shoulder. No leer in *his* voice. Only disapproval.

"But the last name on it," she reminded them, "is Ronald Wendolyn's."

"This is a gag," Riley said. "According to this, the chick even slept with George Washington."

"He was . . . a student."

Allen stood, placed his suitcase flat on the bed, and unsnapped the locks. He pulled out an envelope and sorted through its contents. He handed her a Xerox copy of a newspaper article. An article with the same photograph that had been used on the book jacket. It was Wendolyn's obituary.

She read his list of accomplishments. "Impressive," she said.

"He was a faggot," Riley said.

"You see"—Allen took it from her—"he *is* dead."

"Explain the diary, then. And his name on that list."

"I can't explain it," Allen said.

"What about . . . what about the murder? Do you have something about that?"

He gave her a sheet which contained another photo. The picture of a girl, young and smiling. Her senior-class picture, Diana thought. She read the text with its lengthy account of the beating the girl had received. She thought that she would suffocate on her rising fear.

Allen seemed to sense it. He reached out and squeezed her shoulder. "He was never accused. He was never even suspected."

"But you said . . ."

"Yes." He reached deep into the envelope and extracted a pendant. A golden sunburst, hammered by hand, on a thin gold chain.

She reached for it. "What is it?"

184

"I think it's the same necklace that the girl is wearing in this photograph. It's very hard to tell in this copy, but Paul has the original clipping. Paul?"

They turned to look at Riley. He was reading the Wendolyn obituary, gloating over it, it seemed.

"I don't understand," Diana said, "how this necklace links Wendolyn to the girl."

"Oh, simple," Allen said. "I found it in Wendolyn House. On the mantel over the fireplace. No one, apparently, ever dusted the mantel very carefully."

She considered this. "If Wendolyn murdered the girl, why wouldn't he have taken this with him? Done away with the evidence?"

"But there's more." He brought forth the confession, darkened his voice, and read: "*I, Ronald Wendolyn, did murder Christine Rivers.*"

"Sheesh," Riley said.

Diana swallowed. "We'll have to go to the police. We'll have to."

"Diana. Can you imagine us turning up with all these bits and pieces? Can you imagine what they'd say? It happened in New Hampshire. It might as well have been another country. And not only is the wench dead, but the alleged murderer as well."

"I'm afraid for Lida," Diana reminded him. "I'm really afraid."

"We'll find her." He took the diary and read the entry again. "And it would seem that we'll find her at *The Play of Herod*."

They sat in silence. Diana broke it finally. "You're thinking of something, Allen. What is it?"

"I was thinking that Lida mightn't be in any danger. After all, he *is* on her list. Surely Wendolyn wouldn't kill a woman he was taking to his bed."

"You don't think he was sleeping with that girl?"

"Well, from what Paul has said about him . . ."

185

Riley looked up.

Allen continued. "I hate to get really clinical about this, but the article did say that no traces of semen were found."

"Hey," Riley interjected, "have you two ever heard of rubbers?"

48

Murder. Just like that, out of the blue. Murder. Who would have figured it? He rubbed his knuckles and leaned back to think about it. The sound of it. The feel of it. A grin took over his face.

49

"Who is it?" Duvivier called, though he knew. He tossed his notebook under the bed.

"Renata Tebaldi. I have a singing telegram."

He opened the door. "Come," he said.

"Is that all men ever think about?" Lida wrapped her arms around his neck and spoke with her lips brushing his. "Women, you see, are process-oriented. As opposed to goal-oriented."

"Take your coat off," he said, stepping aside to help her with it.

"It's supposed to snow tonight. I hope they won't cancel the play."

"Yes." He spoke with artificial solemnity. "It would be a great pity to be stranded here in a hotel room together."

She giggled. "How much time do we have?"

"A couple of hours."

"Good." She began to undress.

"How would you like to spend them?"

"In bed," she said. "Why do you think I'm taking my clothes off?"

"Yes, but *how* in bed?"

"How?"

"In your fantasies, how?" He stepped out of his shorts. "I could take you savagely. Or softly. Or not at all."

"Oh, God." She caught hold of his arm and undid the buttons that gave him so much trouble. "The ultimate perversion."

"I mean it. I could hold you. Comfort you. Just that, if you like." A nice touch, he thought. He would add it later.

"What about you?" She lay back on the bed, smiling. "Your fantasies. Because, frankly, you've already fulfilled all of mine."

"I have none. Remember, I'm an old man." He laughed at himself.

"You're holding back, aren't you?" She stretched her arms over her head so that her breasts, small to begin with, all but disappeared. Had she thought of Danielle at this moment, it would have been with gratitude.

"Holding back?" He felt a little burst of fear, as if he had heard the hammer of a gun cocked.

"Yeah."

"I'm not sure I know what you mean."

"Don't you?" She smiled again.

He straddled her waist, then lowered his buttocks onto her stomach. "All right. What *do* you mean?"

She ran her fingers through the hair on his chest, then lightly along his arms.

"Am I too heavy?" he asked.

She shook her head. "Not yet." She brought her hands to rest on his thighs. He began stroking his testicles with his left

189

hand, looking down at her all the while. "Go ahead," she said.

"Aren't you afraid?" he asked. "Doesn't this, in some way, offend you?"

"You mean, do I feel like a prop?"

"Yes."

"If you'd come up a little bit, I wouldn't have to be a prop. I could be a participant."

"Come up?"

"Closer." She tugged at his legs. "Come closer."

"I'm not sure this is anatomically possible."

"Let's find out."

"You've never done this?" He was half-afraid she had.

"No."

"For some reason, that pleases me. Does it please you that I never have?"

"Yes"—she began laughing—"except that you've lost your erection."

"It's all this technical talk," he said, placing a knee beside each of her shoulders. "Here"—he balanced over her—"can you reach?"

She raised her head slightly and ran her tongue over his testicles.

His penis swelled at once. He wrapped his hand around it and began to masturbate. He closed his eyes, fearing he would come too soon.

She blew softly at his testicles, then enveloped them, one by one, in her mouth. "Mmmm," she said, letting his pubic hair tickle her cheek, her nose. "Come in my hair, come on my eyelids, come in my mouth." Her voice, like butter.

He groaned, stiffening, almost falling. Semen splashed across her face, her lips. When it was over, he wiped her face with his hands. "Lida," he whispered, "Lida." He raised his fingers to his lips and sucked at them. "Bitter," he said.

"Warm and bitter."

He swung his leg across her body and stretched out

facedown beside her. "God," he said, "I can't move." But he rolled over and pulled her up against his chest. He stroked her hair, the back of her neck, her shoulders. "Peaceful," he said. "I feel so peaceful."

❧

He must have fallen asleep. He opened his eyes, wondering, for a brief instant, where it was he had awakened. Yes. The hotel. Lida.

He listened. "A bath?" he called.

"I'm all sticky," she shouted over the sound of running water.

He went into the bathroom and sat on the edge of the tub. Steam had fogged the mirror. She lay, her flesh bright pink, amid a cloud of steam. "It's too hot," he commented.

"No, it isn't." She splashed water over her face.

"Your hair," he said.

"What about my hair?"

"It'll get wet."

"Right." She held her nose and leaned back, her head disappearing beneath the surface of the water.

He counted the seconds.

She emerged, still holding her nose. Her hair was sleeked back, flat and shiny against her head.

"You can't go out like that," he said. "You'll get sick."

"I do it all the time," she told him, "and I'm not dead yet."

He moved aside when she climbed out of the tub. He took a towel and began to pat her back, her arms. She took it from him, drying her legs, her feet, her crotch. She dropped it on the floor.

"Sit down," he said, taking a fresh towel.

She sat on the toilet. "I'm not going to pee," she teased.

"I know." He rubbed the towel against her hair, gently, then briskly, then gently again. He tossed the towel aside and

191

bent down, kissing her shoulder. He knelt at her feet, wrapping his arms around her hips. "Lida," he said, kissing her thighs. "Lida, Lida," again and again. He laid his cheek against the brush of her pubic hair and was silent.

"Hey," she whispered, "we've got to go." But she held him. He didn't move.

"Come on," she said again, still whispering. Then her voice neared its normal pitch. "Hey," she said, "what is this? The *Penthouse* version of the pietà?"

"Where is your car," he asked, "in the lot downstairs?"

"No," Lida told him, "my car is in hock. We'll have to take a cab."

"In hock?"

"Too many tickets. It's not worth explaining."

He held her coat. "I saw a hideous production of *Herod* once. A long time ago. This one, I hope, will atone for it."

"At Murdock College?"

He tilted his head a bit to one side. "Yes."

"I've never seen it," Lida said, "but isn't *Herod* a bit before your time?"

"Meaning?"

"You were in Renaissance, not Medieval, right?"

"There's some overlap," he said, checking to make certain that he had his wallet. "The pageantry and what-not. Are you ready?"

50

Scaffolding stretched over the west face of the cathedral, all along the Wisconsin Avenue side. "This thing has been under construction," Lida said, "for as long as I can remember. But it does keep the little men who carve the gargoyles off the street."

The cabdriver grabbed a look at her in his rearview mirror.

"You can buy a gargoyle," she went on, "but you can't take him home with you. He has to stay here. I think they put a little plaque under him, though, so everyone knows he's yours."

"What are gargoyles selling for these days?"

The cabdriver shifted his weight a bit, so that he could glimpse Duvivier as well. A couple of loonies, that's what he had back there.

"Eight hundred and fifty dollars," Lida said.

"That's not bad. Considering that gargoyles are an endangered species."

The cab halted beside a low stone wall. "Is here okay?"

Duvivier counted his change, then put his billfold away.

"They also sell crockets," Lida told him.

"What"— he caught her hand and led her toward a slow-moving file of people—"is a crocket?"

"I don't know. I always meant to find out." She pulled back, opposing his motion. "Hey," she said, "let's go down here." An entrance labeled "Bethlehem Chapel."

"Why?"

"Because they probably have a bathroom down there."

"Go," he said, "I'll follow."

He pulled at his trousers, even though the wind, whipping at them, would have done the job.

He looked at the National Cathedral. It made the people look so small.

He didn't really want to go inside. It was better out here. Here, he could watch the people.

Two nuns went in, arm in arm. They were wearing those new uniforms, so that he could see their legs. One of them really wasn't half-bad.

He thought about what it would be like to fuck a nun. And then really mess her up afterward.

Lida had been right. A small arched door with great hinges upon it. And a plastic sign reading "Ladies." He imagined her ducking inside.

There was a scuffle in the hall, and then the Angel Choir appeared, giggling, poking and punching each other, sliding on the gray marble floor as if it were ice. One of the boys

194

hiccuped. But when they saw him, they stiffened and were silent. Angelic, in fact.

He leaned against the wall uneasily. He never wore a watch, and so had none to look at. But clearly the scene called for a watch, to be consulted at thirty-second intervals.

"My God"— Lida emerged, still fastening her belt—"if it isn't the Heavenly Host."

The boys laughed and tripped away, skidding around a corner and out of sight.

Lida alternately hummed and sang.

Duvivier looked at her questioningly.

"Jimi Hendrix," she said.

The question in his eyes remained.

" 'Electric Ladyland'," she said. "Aw, never mind."

But she continued to hum the song as they took the first staircase, which, according to the placard, would take them to the north transept.

"I want to know how you found my real name," he interrupted.

"And I'll tell you, I promise." And then she hummed some more.

"Would you like to sit in the balcony?" the woman at the table asked.

"Yes!" Diana blurted. "We'll have a better chance of finding them from there."

Allen smiled at the woman as reassuringly as he could. "Yes, the balcony," he said, placing a twenty-dollar bill on the table.

He gathered his change in two clumps, stuffing the bills into his left pocket, then the coins into his right.

He took Diana's arm and leaned toward her. "We could be wrong, Diana. Get hold of yourself." But he knew they weren't wrong. He knew it enough to have stationed Riley, like a sentry, in the vestibule.

"Wrong? No, we can't be wrong. It fits together, all of it."

They took seats along the rail, where everyone in the nave could be seen, though from behind and at a great distance. The others, the ones in general admission, sat in the north and south transepts.

℘

" . . . and then I said, 'Aren't we *all*?' " She paused and noticed that Duvivier wasn't laughing. "Are you sure you want to hear all this?" She asked. "I mean, it's pretty boring."

"Go on," he said, "go on." What, he wondered, *was* a temporary? And how could anyone so designated know anything, much less that he, Duvivier, was or had been Ronald Wendolyn?

"Well, she *didn't* know, silly," Lida explained. "All that *she* did was send me the list of all your books. Under whatever pseudonym. And when I couldn't find *Renaissance Stagecraft* along with your biggies—in the bookstores, I mean . . . "

The story came together now. He didn't need to hear the rest. Of course. He'd been so anxious, in those days, to impress. He couldn't, there on the publicity form, leave the column demanding "Previous Publications" blank. And so he'd written in the title *Renaissance Stagecraft* with a firm backhand stroke. It hadn't been a lie. Just a little something that would show Seare and Jolly—and their charming employee dispensing the forms—that this Duvivier was no fledgling.

But Carol Bradley—the charming employee of the moment—hadn't even looked at the sheet. She'd merely tossed it to the bottom of the folder and proffered another. And then she'd done that thing with her chewing gum.

And there, in the gullet of the Seare and Jolly publicity department, the form had lain. Until regurgitated, at Lida's request, by some temporary. What a mess to clean!

Lida didn't see his frown. " . . . guessed Ronald Wendolyn rather than Bishop—you'd told me about Grisone,

196

remember?—because the Wendolyn book came out in the sixties, and the others . . . "

Guessed Wendolyn rather than Bishop. Guessed it. Duvivier turned to watch her wrap the story up. "Lucky, huh?" was how she tied the bow.

"Oh, God, we'll never find them," Diana said. She tried to remember Lida's various coats, but could only think of two. She looked for someone in a fur jacket. Or someone wearing a green wool coat with a hood. She tried to remember what Wendolyn looked like, but could conjure only that mouth of his. Tight, cruel. The mouth of a murderer.

"Our seats are in the nave, I think." He gave the tickets to an usher, who led them to the third row.

"Whew!" Lida whistled, "the big ten-buck seats, eh?"

He handed her a program absentmindedly. He had already begun to read his own.

Lida folded it and placed it in her purse. She turned around, looking toward the rear of the church.

"Counting the house?" he asked, without looking up from his reading.

"No. I want to see the rose window. It's brand-new and world-famous. A real dazzler."

"Who did it?" He twisted in his chair.

"Who knows?"

"I think we'll have to come back in the morning to see it," he said.

Just then the lights faltered, then fell. *The Play of Herod* began.

Darkness. And then the rustle of bells, fragile in the vast, vaulted hall. The procession of players moved toward the

197

stage in a shiver of candlelight. Sturdy male voices channeled down the left aisle, and from the right, the spare song of the women.

"It's too dark," Diana whispered. "I can't see."

The man behind her cleared his throat pointedly.

"Allen," she said, "I can't see!" With the last word her whisper broke.

A sibilant wave of protest behind, and then a tap on her shoulder. "Madam," the man said, "some of us would like to *hear!*"

The antiphon resolved and the voices joined. Diana would have thought it wonderful had she heard. But all of her energy, all of her concentration, was taken up by her search. She strained against the railing.

A splinter of light. The archangel, wings wide, in lean tenor prophecy: *"Nolite timere vos!"*

Allen found the irony wan. He looked to see if Diana, too, had translated the words: Be no more affrighted.

She had not.

The spotlight illuminated the manger. And in it, Mary and the Babe. Behold! The shepherds were singing, their Latin scrupulous, a virgin shall conceive and bear a son.

"Ever notice," Lida whispered in his ear, cupping her hand over her mouth, "how virgins always smirk?"

Gloria in excelsis Deo!
et in terra pax hominibus
bonae voluntatis

The Angel Choir, frail, boyish, childishly solemn.

Alleluja! Alleluja!

198

A long, hollow pause. And then two voices lifted and entwined, fluid. Ethereal threads spun skyward:

Alle–psallite cum–luja!
Alle–concrepando psallite cum–luja!
Alle–corde voto Deo toto psallite cum–luja!
Alleluja!

"Allen," Diana said, "I can't stand it!"

The Angel Choir again, to sing the second Gloria. But just as they began, a ragged alien voice came from behind. It bounded through the hall. "Lida," it called.

Lida turned and stared into the darkness.

"Lida, he's a murderer!"

The choir went on, as though it hadn't happened. And Lida rose, wondering if she had imagined it. "I . . . "

Alleluja! Alleluja!

She looked to see if Duvivier had heard.

He had. He was gone.

The troupe of actors and musicians paraded past him, a smear of bright color and bright sound. Duvivier waited until they had gone and then slipped silently through the corridors. At his back the music frolicked, faint, then fainter still. In mocking merriment.

And then he was outside, in the chill night quiet.

Lida made her way up the center aisle, reaching the midpoint just as the players turned and started toward her. The man with the recorder spotted her, and played with his eyes wide, moving to the side to make way.

The woman with the vielle followed, giving Lida a sour stare. Lida gave the bagpiper a shove, and broke into a run amid a flurry of cymbals, tambourines, and jingles.

❦

"No, she's quite all right," Allen was telling a little knot of people. "Thanks very much. We're leaving now. Yes, thank you."

Diana leaned against him, like a rag doll.

"What the hell is going on?" Lida asked.

Riley, with sullen interest, watched her approach.

Diana stretched both hands forward. "Oh," she said, "oh, Lida!"

"Hey"—Lida touched Diana's hair—"whatever it is, it's okay now." She looked at Allen and Riley, distributing her distaste equally. "Who are these creeps?" she asked.

51

Lida stared into the coffee they had ordered for her. The clippings lay in disarray beside her saucer.

"I'm so very sorry," Diana said, wiping at her nose with a knuckle.

"I'll be all right. I always recover, don't I?" But she spoke in a furry voice, a voice smaller than any Diana had heard from her.

Riley and Allen watched.

"You can come with us," Diana urged, "talk about it."

But Lida shook her head. "No. I know I do that a lot, Diana, but shit . . ." She sighed, raising her shoulders and letting them fall. "I don't know. I just want to drive. I just want to drive, all by myself. Haven't you ever felt that way?"

Diana smiled. Yes, she had felt that way.

"The thing is," Allen said, "you might not be safe. Wendolyn might be waiting for you." He wished he hadn't had to say it, but it seemed a possibility.

"Fat chance," Lida said.

"I doubt it, too, Allen. He'd have to flee, don't you think?"

"I suppose." Allen furrowed his brow, unsure. "You didn't catch sight of him, did you, Paul?"

"Told you," Riley said, "no."

Allen made up his mind. "Yes, I guess that's what he *would* do. Of course."

They sat in silence, all of them watching Lida.

It was in one of Duvivier's books that Lida had learned about thieves. The good ones, he'd written, did it with aplomb. No furtive glance, no pause. Perhaps a simple diversion to speed things along.

Lida lifted her cup and made a face. "This is too cold," she said, putting the cup back in its saucer. Some of the coffee lapped over the side. Lida tipped the saucer with a very lucky elbow. And a brown pool formed and spread.

They all stood at once. Lida moved the clippings out of range. Allen and Diana dabbed at the tabletop with their napkins. Riley dug in his pockets for his handkerchief. And Lida slid Wendolyn's confession of murder into the pocket of her coat.

"I'm sorry," Lida said when they'd resumed their seats.

"It's fine," Diana told her.

"I'll order another cup," Allen offered, taking the clippings, straightening them. The little gold sunburst slid to the tabletop.

"No, I'd better go." Lida pulled her coat over her shoulders. "But, hey. Would you mind if . . . I know it seems silly, but could I take that?" She pointed at the necklace. "I just want to think about this awhile."

"Of course." Allen pushed at it with his finger, sliding it toward her.

Lida picked it up, clenched her fist around it. "Thanks," she said.

202

"Lida . . . " Diana tugged at her sleeve. "You'll come to my house in the morning?"

"I will. I promise, I will." And then she turned and walked away.

She walked, Diana thought, like someone in mourning. Without thinking, she let her hand slide across the seat until it touched Allen's thigh. It must be awful for Lida, she thought, to have found someone special at last. And then learn—oh, God—that he was a murderer.

"I'll see that she gets to her car," Riley said, standing.

Diana felt guilty, as though she were relinquishing her duty.

Allen lifted her hand, placed it square on his thigh, and covered it with his own hand. "Good idea, Paul," he said.

They watched Riley move toward the door. "Is it a good idea?" she asked.

Allen looked at her quizzically.

"It's just that I don't like him," she admitted. "I don't like the way he thinks about Lida. The way he was about that list."

"Would you prefer that she be with Wendolyn?"

She thought for a moment. "Yes, almost that."

He shook his head. "Call your sons," he said. "Tell them they'll have to manage the night without you."

She paused.

"They're old enough."

"Where's the phone?" she asked, but then she spied a sign that pointed to a staircase.

"I'll come with you," he said.

"No. There will be a long argument from which I'll just barely emerge the victor. I don't want you to witness any of it."

"I'll be waiting, then," he said. "I'll pay the bill and meet you just outside." He watched her go.

52

Duvivier considered the great bulk of the National Cathedral. It reassured him. A thousand places to hide, if it came to that. He walked the grounds, wondering what he should do.

There were patrolmen everywhere, probably to direct the masses who had come to see *The Play of Herod*. Amazing, that such an esoteric event should draw so many. Perhaps he had underestimated that great body which e. e. cummings tagged "mostpeople."

He was annoyed with the meanderings of his mind, bothered that he should traverse scholarly byways now, in what was clearly a time of peril.

Yet he was curiously relaxed. He walked, in fact, so slowly as to draw no attention from the uniformed guards. A wise move, though not in the least deliberate.

Klieg lights played on the hulking Gothic structure now some distance behind him. Safe to hurry up some now.

'Q'

Even though he hadn't covered more than half a block, his breath was coming fast and loud, like the breath of a kid who's just stopped crying. It was the cold. That made it worse.

But all of a sudden it got better. All of a sudden she was there.

She had crossed from shadow into the halo of a streetlamp. And there, like magic, she stood. She fumbled with her collar. She fastened the chain. And the necklace shone an eerie gold against her coat. She patted her pocket. She smoothed her hair.

But when he'd almost made it to where she had appeared . . . It *was* like magic.

But she'd made sure that he heard. The little cunt—she was asking for it.

He leaned against a parked car, still breathing hard. The Watergate. Christ, she still had quite a sense of humor.

'Q'

Lida ransacked her bag, hoping she had enough money to pay the fare. "Is there some kind of light back here?" she asked.

A small yellow overhead came on.

Nail polish. Perfume. Keys. *Lolita*. Three wadded Kleenex. The spermicidal jelly. Where the hell was her wallet? She found it, counting the bills. There were a ten and seven ones.

"Got enough?" the cabbie said, eyeing her in the rearview mirror.

"Just drive."

"You're real friendly," he said.

"Can you go any faster?"

205

"Not me. They give tickets in this town to everyone. Cabs. Probably buses, too. It's murder."

"Yeah," Lida said, wondering how much time had gone by, "I know what you mean." Would he be gone when she got there? And if he hadn't gone, what then?

That friend of hers had told her all of it by now. Or all of what she knew. He could only fare worse in her limited version.

Had Lida shuddered as she heard? Waxed white, thinking of the dangers she had passed? He grieved for those dangers, pitied them, in fact.

Yet how might he have described the death of that girl to the New Hampshire police? To anyone? Even to Lida. Too ridiculous for words.

"Well, actually,"—he imagined himself, a veritable Cyrano, addressing the jury—" she died *in flagrante delicto*. Come to think of it, ladies and gentlemen, you should take care not to translate that literally. Literally, you would have to say that she died *in flagrante defatigo*." He would lean across the wooden panel, winking at the third juror from the right. "Do you know what I mean?"

There could be no other plan. He would go back to the hotel. And then to the airport. Then back across the ocean.

He reached into his pocket for the key. And then he remembered that Lida had it. He pictured the police, bending over Lida's broken body, then examining the contents of her bag. And there it would be, glittering in the revolving red light: the link, direct and irrefutable.

He shook his head in disgust, then beckoned to a cruising cab.

53

A twist of the knob. And then Duvivier stood in the doorway.

Lida sat at the desk, polishing her nails. She held her left hand aloft, and with the right, applied the enamel.

"That would be a very effective scene," he told her, "if your hands weren't shaking."

"Funny," she said. "I was just thinking the same thing."

He crossed the room and stood beside her. "Why *are* they shaking?"

"I don't know," she lied. She laid her left hand on the flat surface and braced the right by resting her forearm against the edge of the desk.

He smiled. "There. You've stopped shaking."

"No. I've just got some leverage now."

He sighed and sat on the edge of the bed, thinking of what she'd said.

She replaced the brush in the little bottle, waving her fingers about. "No heavy meaning, honest. I was talking about my nails."

"You thought you were." His voice lacked energy.

"They told me you were dead."

He laughed. "They may be right." He glanced at the necklace, and watched her throat as she swallowed.

"I'd put my arms around you," Lida said, "if my nails were dry. Despite the fact that they think you're a murderer." She nudged his confession toward him with her elbow.

He took it, read, and laid it back again.

She looked at her fingers, tested one of the nails. "Too bloody red, if you ask me. Do you agree?" She held up a hand.

"Does your friend know where you are?" he asked.

"No."

"Is there any way she could find you? Could she have followed you here?"

"No." She answered his questions without hesitation.

"Are you going to complicate this," he said, covering his face with his hands, "by trusting me?"

"Worse," Lida said.

He spread his fingers and looked at her between them.

That necklace, glittering in the foreground. Behind it, Lida's features had faded and dissolved.

And when the focus returned, she had changed. Was younger, brassier. Her nose had altered too. It was slightly tilted now. Just the way that he remembered it.

So long ago.

"Look, I had to come back," Lida told him. "I was out of cigarettes."

208

"I have some. They're over there." He looked over at the bureau.

"Yes." She laughed. "I watched you take them out of your pocket. You stood there"—she jumped up and pivoted before the mirror—"looking at the lump they made in your pocket. And then you took them out and put them there." She patted the package.

"I was choosing between my vanity and my vice. As a matter of fact, that line ran through my mind while I was doing it. But I didn't know that you were watching."

"What if you had known?"

"Oh, then I'd have been very cavalier about it. Probably wouldn't have checked the mirror at all."

She lit a cigarette and offered it to him.

"No," he said, "you go ahead." He watched her inhale. "You smoke like Bette Davis."

"I've practiced," she answered, going back to the mirror and watching herself maneuver the cigarette.

"Didn't you tell me—yes, in your letter—that you were planning to quit?" He came beside her and took the cigarette. He drew on it, and then put it back in her hand. "Well?"

"I probably said that. I am planning to quit."

He put his arm around her and posed beside her, Grant Wood fashion. "But if you quit," he said, admiring their reflection, "what will you do after lovemaking? I mean, what do people who don't smoke *do* after they've made love?"

Lida looked at him. She would have said "sex" or "fucking." But maybe he always said that. "If they're middle-aged," she said, breaking away and sitting on the bed, "they eat cupcakes. And if they're groovy young couples, they have sea toast. Or crunchy granola."

"In either case, it makes for a gritty bed." He stooped and lifted her legs, unzipping the boots that she wore. He pulled them, let them thud to the carpet.

"Do my feet smell?" she asked.

"Horribly." He kissed them. He ran his hand along her leg

until it bumped against her hemline. "This isn't a skirt, is it?" he asked.

"No," she said.

"How does it come off?"

"Not easily." She stood and undid the belt and the buttons at her waist. She slid it over her hips, catching her pantyhose as well, stepping free.

"What do you call it? A pant-skirt?"

"You call it culottes or gauchos or something. And you use the plural."

"I'll remember that," he said, sitting before her on the bed and kissing her stomach. "Here . . ." He stood and turned her around. "You lie down." Then he spread her legs and licked at her, sliding his hands under her sweater and along her sides as he did so.

Lida closed her eyes, thinking that it must have taken thousands of women to bring him to this expertise. And glad, so glad, that she was one of them.

"What are you thinking?" he asked after a long while.

"I was wondering if you would do this to me if I were menstruating."

"You are menstruating," he said, lowering his head again.

Hundreds of thousands of women. "What was it like the first time?" she asked.

"Your're crazy," he said, biting her thigh. "Go to sleep."

But seconds later she was . . . oh, God, oh, *God!* So awake!

His kisses were vaguely metallic. "Are you sure I'm menstruating?" Lida asked. "Maybe I'm rusting." She squirmed away.

"Where are you going?" he asked.

"I want to make sure I have Tampax."

"You have," he said. "I saw them in your bag."

"I want to count them," she insisted. "And anyway, why

don't you take advantage of this moment and undress. Your belt buckle was killing me."

"Don't tell me what to do," he said.

She stopped counting and looked at him. "Did you mean that? What you just said?"

"No. I was trying out the line. It sounded awfully macho, don't you think?" He raised himself with a heavy sigh and began to remove his clothing. "It wouldn't work, though."

"Why not?"

"Don't be silly. What man would resent a woman ordering him to take his clothes off?" He watched her tear the wrapper from the tampon. "What are you doing?" he asked. "You aren't going to put that in?"

"If I don't, the bed will look as though some bitch has had a litter of puppies in it."

"Oh, Lida," he said, embracing her. "You're such good copy." He took the tampon from her hand and held it between his fingers as though it were a cigar. "Say the magic word," he said, his brows bobbing, "and the duck will come down and give you a hundred dollars."

"Not this duck, Groucho," she said, shoving him back on the bed. "This duck has something else in mind."

Lida heard the strike of his match and wondered how long he had been awake. "Do you want a cigarette?" he asked her.

"No," she said, sliding her arm across the bed until it touched some part of him.

"Did you sleep?" He laid his hand on her ass.

"I think so."

He took his hand away. She heard the scrape of the ashtray and the sound of his cigarette tapping against it. She waited.

He leaned over her, his lips damp across her back. "I hope you won't be lonelier tomorrow because of this," he said.

"No."

"But you will be. I can tell."

"All right, yes." Tomorrow, she thought, and for the rest of my life.

Lida rolled over to face him, stretching. The necklace tangled in her hair.

He reached for it and gently tugged it free. He unraveled the chain to its fullest extent. The sunburst rested above her breasts.

"I thought you took this off," he said, tracing its outline with his finger.

"I don't remember taking anything off." She closed her hand over his.

"Come on," he said. "Get up. It must be after ten."

Look at her standing there. That necklace. And that throat of hers, so long, so white.

> If you were queen of pleasure
> And I were king of pain . . .

Christ, yes. His fingers on that throat, that white skin going blue under his touch. Just like old times.

"You wait here," he told her, settling Lida beside a potted palm. "I'll take care of the bill."

She watched him walk to the counter, his posture heroic. It was, she knew, because he sensed that she was watching.

The desk clerk slid the account sheet toward him and Duvivier read it, lifting his spectacles slightly, sliding them along his nose. On another man, Lida noted, the gesture would have seemed professorial, and too consciously so.

The clerk drummed his fingertips on the edge of the

212

counter. "It isn't the Magna Carta, sir," he would like to have said. He was a sophomore at George Washington University, and had recently declared Early European History as his major. But the flurry of cash which Duvivier conferred upon him quelled any would-be sarcasm. And when Lida appeared at Duvivier's side, the clerk was forced to give Duvivier a few more points.

"If you've got any money left over," Lida said, "let's do Howard Johnson's. For old times' sake."

<p>

The desk clerk watched Duvivier guide Lida through the crowded lobby. Yeah. He'd do it like that tonight, with Sheila. Take her hand, look at her, tack this way and that, parting the people like they were the Red Sea and he was Moses. The guy had style. Not like the creep who went out right behind them. The one with his pants stuck in the crack of his ass.

<p>

He pulled one of the doors wide, and Lida walked through. The smell of coffee rushed at them, as though trying to escape into the street. He might have said that to Lida, but she had already moved to the rail and taken a tray. He watched her start down the cafeteria line.

She stopped at a section where steam had clouded the glass between her and the food. She stood on tiptoe and peered over the barrier at the selection. Then she lifted her gaze to read the menu posted overhead.

Duvivier turned his attention to the dining room.

An old man and a child sat across from each other at a booth near the window. The man had hung his coat, but a bright plaid scarf was still wrapped around his neck. The boy wore an oversized jersey with a number emblazoned across the back. At a corner table in the rear, two uniformed policemen stirred their coffee. Their hats dangled from a rack behind them.

The boy talked, calling the old man "Gramps." He mentioned the White House and asked his grandfather if he would like to live there. The officers in the corner conversed, too, but in low tones punctuated with laughter. Perhaps they also were discussing the presidency.

The other patrons—six, at most—were scattered at single tables throughout the room. One read *The Washington Post*, unaware of the coffee stain that was spreading steadily on his tie. Another perused a comic book, bracing it against a napkin stand. A thin, dark-haired girl sat reading what seemed to be a letter. She had chosen a table with a floral arrangement: a single plastic rose stuck inside a tumbler. She was wistful, chewing at a piece of toast.

He walked along inside the rail until he stood behind Lida. "You're holding up the line, madam," he said, taking her by the waist.

She gave her tray a little shove and tilted her head to feel his breath against her neck. And then she turned. "Aren't you going to get a tray?" she asked.

"I'll use yours," he said. "I don't want very much." But he puzzled at the way her body tensed. "What is it?" he asked.

"Go get us a booth, will you?" she said hurriedly. "Way in the back."

"But . . ."

"Do it, okay? I want to surprise you."

He took a ten from his pocket and laid it on the tray. He moved away uncertainly.

Something odd about her manner. Perhaps he had offended her. Perhaps he should have taken a tray of his own.

He sat at the only clean table he could find, across from the police. Would she remember that the last time they were here, he'd found the orange juice too sweet?

Lida cursed her own stupidity. They had let her go too easily last night. She knew that now. God, she was a dope.

She looked over at Duvivier and swallowed hard. He was staring at the cops, or past them, she couldn't tell. Had the cops been planted there? Probably. And she had sent Duvivier almost to their very table.

God, she was a dope.

She looked back into the street, hoping she'd been wrong about the face she'd seen there. But she wasn't wrong. And Diana was probably right behind him, with the whole D.C. police force in tow. Shit. And what would Diana say? That it had been for Lida's own good. What did *she* ever know?

And what would Duvivier say? That she, Lida, had done it. She, Lida, had betrayed him.

God, she was a dope.

He hit both doors at once and they opened with a loud rush of air. He stepped inside, just beyond their range. He was looking dead at Lida. Behind him, the doors closed slowly, the left ahead of the right.

Lida waited for Diana to appear, with her uniformed entourage. The clatter of cups against saucers, the clank of forks against plates, went on without pause. The little boy still prattled at his grandfather, and off in the corner, the cops continued their dialogue.

The man stretched his hand toward Lida. "You little bitch," he said. "God damn you. You little bitch." He had begun quietly, his voice almost tender. But it altered as he spoke. The last word was a bleat.

There was a railing between them. Lida was glad of that.

"All right, so I lied and went to him anyway." Lida said. She gave a little shrug. "But so what?"

"Bitch," he murmured.

"Hey, wait a minute." Lida held up her hand. "In the first place, it's none of your business. And in the second place, where's Diana? I would rather talk to her about this."

"It is my business, baby. It sure is my business."

She imagined them breaking into a childish routine.

"No it isn't," she would say.

"Yes it is," he would answer.

And it would go on and on like that. The thought made Lida laugh.

"Are you laughing at me, you bitch?"

Everyone heard. The space grew between one noise and the next. And then the conversations died utterly. Now there was only a hissing sound from somewhere behind the counter.

Above that sound, Lida's voice quavered. "Where's Diana?" she repeated, knowing as she spoke that Diana wasn't there, wasn't coming. This was something else, but what?

"It's so hard to make you cry," he said to Lida, "but I'll make you cry. Oh, I'll make you cry. Didn't I make you cry last time? Didn't I?" He crooned the words as though they were part of a liturgy. A ritualized seduction.

Duvivier had risen involuntarily. But he could not have moved farther. He could only stand, his fingers pressed flat on the table, an incredible heaviness filling his joints, his muscles. He could not believe what he was seeing.

"Last time," Lida whispered, her hand groping for the sunburst on the chain. She thought he'd been staring at her tits, but no. It was there, at the necklace, he'd been staring.

"Come on," he chanted. "Come on, Christine."

Christine!

Duvivier felt as though a huge, Kong-like fist had closed

around him. It squeezed just once, and then it dropped him free.

"Jesus Christ," she had whined behind him, "I think you broke my nose." Christine! In his car that snowswept night. Her prattle rising and falling over and under his consciousness. About how *he* would fix her ass and his ass too. And *he* had. *He* had fixed her ass.

Christine! Why had he never thought of it?

Christine, skipping from his car with a bow. "I bleed, sir, but not killed." Tossing his handkerchief back in through the window. And even as he'd folded it, placed in in his pocket, she was walking toward the spot where Paul Riley waited. Walking toward her appointment with death.

"My God," Duvivier said. He turned toward the table where the cops were sitting. One of them had craned around in his seat to watch, and now was returning to his eggs and bacon; the other hadn't even glanced at the fray. No hope there, Duvivier decided. He would have to do it himself. He walked quickly to the door of the restaurant, hoping to catch sight of them. But it was too late.

"I want to go where the bad man took the lady," the little boy was saying to his grandfather.

Duvivier crouched beside the booth. "Where?" he asked. "Where did the bad man take the lady?"

The little boy looked at him and then across the table to his grandfather. "Is it okay, Gramps?"

The old man nodded.

"To the museum, where there's air and space. The Air and Space museum."

Duvivier rose stiffly. He smiled his sanest smile. He left.

Then he ran like hell.

54

"You were with that faggot again, Christine." Riley's voice was calm now, but artificially so.

Lida wished she'd taken more psych courses in college. She tried vainly to think of the categories, wondering which one he'd fall into.

"You gonna answer me?" He stopped walking and took her face in his hands. then he started squeezing his hands together.

She reached up and caught his arms. The pressure eased. She was able to take his hands away. "But he's a faggot," she said. "Why worry?"

He laughed. They started walking again. Then he stopped laughing and began looking over at her at every other stride.

Now what? Lida wondered. Would he follow them? Could he catch up? But anyway, they were in the streets of the nation's capital, and it was broad daylight.

He stopped.

She stopped as well.

He took her hand and maneuvered her backward, against the face of a building. Then he dropped her hand and pressed his palms against her cheeks again.

People passed them by. Lida heard their heels clicking against the pavement. No one stopped. No one interfered. No one even slowed down.

"Hey . . ." She raised her knee and rubbed it along the side of Riley's leg. "Hey, come on," she said. The pressure of his fingers eased again. His hands moved to her shoulders. And then he placed his hands against the building. Beside her, forming a little cage.

She pointed her toe and rubbed it along his instep, up his calf. "In a little bit," she said.

"At that museum?" he said throatily.

"Mmm, yes."

"You're disgusting." A woman stood beside them and pushed her face toward Lida's. "This is a disgusting display."

Riley dropped his hands. He hung his head.

Where were you, Lida wondered, when he was killing me?

"Wait a minute," Lida said to the woman.

"You're a whore. Don't touch me, you whore." She backed away. She spat on the pavement.

"Maybe we should get a cab," Riley said, still looking down. "I'm sick of walking."

"We'll walk slower." Lida ran her hand along the side of his face. The woman was still there, watching. "Don't you like to walk with me?" she asked.

Without looking up, he slapped her hand away. "Knock it off," he said. "I don't want a bunch of kooks staring at us."

The woman was still watching. Maybe, maybe.

"Ronald Wendolyn walks with me all the time," Lida said.

He grabbed her face again. Grabbed it and squeezed. "You filthy little bitch," he said.

Tears were clogging Lida's vision. But she could see the

woman as a blur. Still there. Coming closer.

Upon them now.

"You see?" The woman's face loomed again. "The Lord will punish you. You see?" She turned and walked away.

Lida took her knee again, and rubbed it over his groin. The son of a bitch. He already had an erection.

But he dropped his hands. "I told you," he said, "not here." He started walking and looked back at her. "Come on, Christine."

55

Duvivier leaned over the balcony opposite the main entrance of the Air and Space Museum. Behind him, like a giant phallus, was the Explorer Two space capsule.

What would he do when he saw them? For a brief moment his imagination usurped his fear. He saw himself vaulting into the open-cockpit plane that dangled from the ceiling. He would toss his scarf over his shoulder and stand, cutting the guy wires that suspended it. Then he would swoop down, in one heroic pass. Paul Riley would be felled by the propeller. And he, Duvivier, would lean over the side of the plane, catching Lida in his arms.

Then he thought of Riley with Lida in the restaurant. "It's so hard to make you cry," he had said, "but I'll make you cry." Oh, God.

Suppose they had already gotten here?

Suppose they came in one of the other entrances?

Suppose they never came at all?

56

The museum was in sight now. It looked as though she would make it, after all. The police would be there. They would grab him as soon as he stepped inside the door. And she would collapse against Duvivier, maybe even cry.

"Are you thinking about him, Christine?"

"About who?"

"You know who."

"No," she said.

"You sure?"

"Yeah, I'm sure." Jesus Christ. Did anyone ever consider that Christine Rivers might have committed suicide?

Duvivier heard Lida before he saw her. He had all but given up. He had started down the floating staircase, the carcass of a

V-2 rocket obstructing his view of the door.

"Not yet," she said with exaggerated petulance. "I want to look around first."

Duvivier waited on the landing as they walked past. And then he followed, gingerly, in their contrails.

Lida stood before a blowup of the surface of the moon. She traced her finger along the edge of a crater, playing for time. Just where the hell were those cops? Did you have to be behind the wheel of a car to bring them out of their hiding hole? But maybe they were there, laid back but ready. Maybe. Lida tried to roll her eyes without moving her head. So that Riley wouldn't notice.

Riley stood behind her, staring at her ass.

Duvivier thought of his heroes. Any one of them would have grabbed Riley by the shoulder, spinning him around. Then they'd send one swift punch to Riley's jaw, toppling him backward, impaling him on one of the jagged moon rocks.

Duvivier could only watch.

They moved into one of the small exhibit cubicles. Duvivier stood at the door, waiting. There were several people in the room, so he was sure Lida would be safe.

Riley stood beside a small Army helicopter. Lida examined it, moving from the cockpit toward the tail. Then around the tail, back along the other side.

Riley kept his eyes on her.

She leaned her hand against the prop. She pushed. It spun around, and the nearest blade hit Riley on the temple.

"That does it," he said, coming after her.

Lida laughed, as if it were a game.

She dodged behind some tourists, and then moved on.

Riley lumbered after her, his face getting redder, his hands reaching forward.

Duvivier moved to block his progress. The door was wide, too wide to bar it with his body. But if he could confront Riley, offering himself in exchange for Lida . . .

Duvivier stood in a pose that mirrored the Crucifixion.

And Riley pushed past him, without recognition.

That scared Duvivier more than anything else had yet.

Lida spotted a queue that had formed for the movie, *Flight.* It was a thick line, with the people standing four abreast. She ran alongside it. Why were there no *guards*? And then she saw the tallest man that she could ever hope to see.

He was a big, loose-jointed black, a basketball player, she supposed. Even without the hair, which was massive, he must have been seven feet tall. The tallest of the others came up to the base of the camera which the man had slung around his neck. It looked like a miniature camera resting on his chest.

Lida aimed for him, connected, and reached up, taking his arm. "Hey, my friend thinks you're just a dumb nigger," she said, "but I think you're cute."

Even before the man's eyes could grow large, Riley was there. He lunged, stretching forward, his hand grabbing for Lida's face.

Lida ducked. Riley caught hold of a thick brown male forearm.

The man glared down at Riley. The top of Riley's head was, maybe, mid-lens. But Riley didn't drop his arm, even though the huge man swung around, stepped forward, facing Riley now.

People began to bob, with everyone straining to see. Lida took a step backward.

And then Riley dropped his arm, and he, too, moved back.

"That's better," the man said, smiling. It wasn't a conciliatory smile. It was mean. "Now, what—exactly—is that you say?"

And Riley stood, heaving, considering. It only took a second, maybe less. Riley brought his leg up, straight, fast, high. It hit the man in the groin, audibly.

Everyone gasped, in chorus.

The huge man fell, clutching his testicles and wailing. He rolled from this side to that, the camera clattering against the floor behind him.

The people swarmed crazily, and Duvivier hopped up on the staircase, the better to see.

The, around the corner from the knot of people, he caught a green flash that registered as Lida's coat. The door to the ladies' room closed behind it.

Lida raced through the room where the mirrors and the sinks were and back into the room with the stalls. There would be a window. She would climb out the window, run through the streets. She was safe now, she thought irrationally. He couldn't follow her here. He wouldn't dare.

There *was* a window. And just behind it, a thick mesh screen. Lida curled her fingers through it, tried to move it, shake it. An impenetrable mesh screen.

The people had not yet resumed their places in the line. The black man was standing now, without his camera. He was stooping to talk to a doddering security guard, who was writing in a little pad.

Duvivier looked back toward the ladies' room, and just in time.

Paul Riley had opened the door. He looked back at the milling crowd just once, and then he went inside.

225

57

It was just a little squeak, the sort that a tiny drop of oil would have remedied. But when Lida heard it, she knew that Riley had opened the outer door.

She slipped into the nearest stall and softly, steadily drew the bolt. She waited for the inner door to open. It did not.

"Christine?" he called from the dressing room beyond. Something tentative, uneasy about his voice.

Of course. Men, even murdering men, do not customarily violate the sanctuary of a women's rest room.

But how long would his reticence last?

She could see him out there in her mind's eye, flexing his hands in anticipation. Paul Riley, purple-faced and breathing hard, his rage multiplied in the row of mirrors that stood above the sinks.

"Christine?" His voice was bolder now.

She squatted on the tile floor, then slid beneath the side of the stall into the next toilet. She locked the door of this one, and slid again, to the third.

She kept on going, until she had reached the farthest stall. There were ten in all. And now, in the last, Lida climbed up on the toilet seat and crouched.

The inner door opened. She did not hear it close. He was standing in the doorway, she guessed, still uncertain.

"Christine?"

℧

Duvivier and the guard stood just outside the entrance to the ladies' room. From within, they could hear him calling.

The guard took the pad from his pocket and wrote: "I will call D.C. police." And then he moved away, leaving Duvivier there alone.

℧

"Come on, Christine." Riley took a step forward.

Lida heard the door. Heard his breath. In the stark tile room, the sound was amplified, the effect was heightened. He was inside now. And what would she do?

"I know you slept around," he said, "but that was okay. You know it was. But you weren't *sleeping* with that faggot, Christine, were you?" Something was tearing at his words. Maybe laughter, maybe tears. Maybe both. "So what were you doing, Christine? What were you doing? Well, you lied to me. You lied. If you slept with him, that would have been okay, but no. I'll tell you what you were doing. I'll tell you."

How long could Lida stay crouched in this position? She dared not stand, because her head would show above the row of stalls. Nor could she ease herself to the floor, because Riley was coming up the row, bending, she could tell, to look under each of the doors.

"You were letting him do it to you, rough you up. And I

227

saw, I saw. You could lie, but I could see." He was weeping now. "We had something good, you and me. Something that was all ours. But you let him, a lousy faggot, do it too. And you let him do your *face*, Christine. Your *face*! You never let me do your face."

He was Lida guessed, at the fourth stall now. Whenever he stopped to look under one of the doors, he stopped talking. There was no other logic to the pauses. It was just that he could not talk and squat at the same time. Like a Polish joke, Lida thought. Inexplicably, she ached to laugh.

"And you let him do your nose. I thought you were saving your nose for me. Your nose." He bawled like a baby. But he kept on coming up the row. "I watched you get out of his car. I saw what you let him do to you."

The guard was back. He opened the outer door and went inside, holding it so that Duvivier could follow. They stood in the dressing room and listened.

The guard carried no gun, but he had drawn a mace. He was a small gray-haired man, withered like a cornstalk in the fall. He looked anything but threatening.

Duvivier would have groaned, except that Riley would have heard.

"You remember, Christine, don't you? You remember what I did to you last time. That really hurt you, didn't it? But this time will be even better." Riley laughed.

The guard handed Duvivier the mace and pulled his pad out, scrawling. "He is not alone in there." Just then the outer door opened.

Lida tried to stretch her hand out to brace herself. If she didn't, she would fall, she was sure of it. And when she stretched her hand out, she realized, with astonishment, that her purse was still draped over her shoulder.

That was very stupid. Or very smart. She reached inside carefully, trying not to make any noise.

Okay, Riley, what will it be? The old ignition keys to the nostril? Why not? He liked noses, after all.

She felt for the keys, found them, and closed her fist around them. She had to be sure that they wouldn't jingle.

But they did. They gave a tinny little rattle that he couldn't help but hear.

Lida heard his footsteps coming toward her. They were heavy and sure. Riley had her now.

The seven-foot black man burst into the room where Duvivier and the guard waited. "Is that cocksucker still in here?" he asked.

Before they could answer, he had gone in after Riley.

"Well, hello there, whitey."

Lida heard him and knew, instantly, who it was. Just beyond the door of the stall where she was hidden, she heard the scrape of Riley's feet. He was turning.

Lida's hand moved convulsively in her purse. What she found was the tube of spermicidal jelly. She took it out, made a cup with her left hand, and squeezed the tube with her right.

The only thing that she could hear now was the sound of the two men breathing. The sound of two men facing each other, squared off for a fight.

God damn it, Riley, she thought. You really *are* crazy.

"You know what I'm gonna make of you, white man? I'm gonna make you into scrapple. I'm gonna take your pig face and your pig guts and I'm gonna make you into scrapple."

229

Lida lowered her feet to the floor, half-expecting someone to reach under the door, grab for her legs. But no one did. She stood and heard the joints of her knees and shoulders crack.

Riley took a shuffling step forward. The black man apparently hadn't moved.

Lida drew the bolt, holding her left hand aloft. The thick, mucoid mass was heaped in her palm and ready. She opened the door and stood there, staring at the heaving back and shoulders of Paul Riley.

☿

He turned his head, sensing her there. And she stepped to the side and slapped her hand upward and over his eyes. Riley screamed. His arms flailed, seeking her, but she pressed her hand hard, kneading with her fingers.

"Oh, come on," Lida said, "it can't hurt—it doesn't burn when you put it *there*." She narrowly dodged his grasp.

Riley staggered against the wall, his hands clapped over his eyes. He wiped frantically. He was still screaming when the black man got to him.

He probably couldn't have seen the huge man standing before him. The immense black hand that opened, catching both his wrists. The same black hand, forcing Riley's hands down and against Riley's own groin. Pressing. And pressing.

Riley stopped screaming and began to sob.

"White man, why you want to hurt yourself this way?" Increasing the pressure against Riley's groin. Until Riley's body shrank against the wall, dropping to the floor.

☿

Lida pressed her cheek against the cool tile wall and listened to the voices that shouted and rang around her. She felt weak—suddenly and utterly—as though someone had, with

230

sleight of hand, yanked her skeleton out from beneath her skin. She shut her eyes.

And then Duvivier materialized beside her. "Ah," he said, his voice jovial, light, admiring. "'She neither swooned nor utterd cry.'"

Lida opened her eyes and slowly turned her gaze and then her head in his direction.

For a long moment he read her face, and then he shrugged and backed away, stepping into one of the stalls. "Tennyson," he called over the crackle of paper. "And not as silly a poem as you think. For instance, there's the line, 'She must weep or she will die.'" He reappeared with several stacks of toilet tissue. He began stuffing them into this pockets as Lida watched. Then he spread his arms, walked toward her. "Do that, Lida." He reached for her, gathered her in, held her. "Weep. Or swoon. Do whatever you like."

Piece by piece, Lida took the tissue from his pockets. Until she had used it all.

58

Lida and Duvivier watched the squad car bearing Riley pull away.

The black man was sitting in the back seat of another squad car, towering above a cop in the front seat. The cop was writing, his head bobbing up and down. The black's huge hands clapped the air as he spoke.

Still another cop was talking to Lida. "Off the top of my head," he said, "I'd say he just kind of clicked over. Looked at you and clicked over. Thought you were his girl." He rustled through his notes. "Christine Rivers?" He looked at Duvivier. "That the name he kept saying?"

"Yes, that's what he kept saying."

"Well, I read the name to the old guy on the security force and he said that was it, too. So if you two will come on down to the station, we can wrap it up."

"What will happen?" Lida asked.

"The guy had a lot of ID. We'll call up there where he lives and check with this Rivers girl. But you know what my feeling is on this?"

"What's that?" Duvivier asked.

"Even if she's *got* charges to press, she won't."

Duvivier agreed. "Domestic stuff," he said.

"That's right," the cop replied, with something like admiration. He turned the look toward Lida. "I gather you were pretty cool in there, miss."

"I watch a lot of television," Lida said.

Lida opened the door of the police station and peered into the street. She smiled when she saw him waiting. "Hey," she said, "how did you get done so fast?"

"I had less to tell," he said.

"Then you didn't go into the whole Wendolyn bit."

"Of course not. Did you?"

"Nope. And I didn't prefer charges, either. Anyhow, you want to hear the name I used? Florinda Cianfrandelli."

"No wonder you were in there so long." He laughed. "But you might have chosen something less flamboyant."

"Oh, yeah? Well, who were you?"

"Bob Bland," he told her.

"Jesus."

"What will happen now?" Lida asked. "You write these things. Tell me."

"I guess they'll call the New Hampshire police, find out about Christine Rivers' murder, and nail Riley for it. What else?"

"And what about Diana and that guy?"

"What guy?"

"I don't know. Some guy who had all the newspaper clippings and shit. The one who brought Riley here. The one who told me you did it."

233

"What was his name?"

"Allen something. Allen Dilworth."

"I've never heard of him."

"Never heard of him!" Lida bellowed. "Jesus Christ!"

Several passersby turned to stare. They quickened their pace, in the event that she was distributing pamphlets. Duvivier took no notice. "Look," he said. "If Dilworth is from the college—and he probably is—he'll find out about Riley when he gets back there. I don't know."

"Well, I want to know," she insisted. "I like a nice, tidy plot. No loose ends. Like Perry Mason."

"But the story has an intrinsic flaw," he told her.

"Which is?"

"That the exquisitely crafter Duvivier . . ."—he ran his thumbs along the lapel of his coat, watching Lida roll her eyes—"should be exonerated of a murder that he hadn't committed to begin with. That anyone so wonderfully conceived could be asshole enough . . ."

"Don't. He's not an asshole."

"No? Well, try this, then." He hyped his presentation of the truth so that, if she laughed at it, he could laugh with her, pretending it had only been a joke all along. "That Duvivier wrote with such strength that even *he* believed the words that he had placed on the page." The wrong words.

"Yes, I like that." She squeezed his hand. "That's probably just what you did."

"You *do* watch a lot of television," he said, smiling at her.

59

"But I must be like her," Lida said.

Duvivier seemed puzzled.

"Like Christine Rivers." The thought made her sad.

"No," he said, "she had a much cuter nose." But when he saw that Lida didn't smile, he stopped walking.

Lida turned. He laid his hands on her shoulders. "You're brash," he said, "as she was. And you're unsettling, as she was. But she was conspicuously sexual. Not like you at all. There was something desperate about her. As though she had some quota that she had to meet, you know, so many men by the end of the year."

"You make me sound like a fucking virgin," Lida said.

"You know what I mean. Only, a man like Riley wouldn't know the difference between someone like her and someone like you."

Or a man like Charles. Or a man like Jerry. I could give you

235

a whole list of names, she thought.

They wandered the streets with no destination.

"Is this vagrancy?" Lida asked.

"I thought it was loafing," he said.

Lida saw a phone booth at the end of the block and led him toward it. "I should call Diana," she said. "I told her I'd be there."

"Go ahead." He plumbed his pockets and produced a handful of change. Lida took it and arranged it on the little metal shelf beneath the phone. "What will you say?" he asked.

"That you didn't do it." Lida pulled the door to the booth shut and dialed.

"She gave us this number," Eddie said, "but she said not to call unless it was an emergency."

"What's the number?"

"Is this an emergency?"

"Yes, god damn it. What's the number?" She kicked the door open and covered the mouthpiece. "I hate kids," she told Duvivier. "Especially Diana's kids."

He saw her lips move, reciting the number over and over again so that she wouldn't forget it.

"What are you doing in some sleazy motel?" she accused Diana. "You're supposed to be at your place, consoling me."

Diana giggled in response. Lida heard her say "It's Lida," to someone in the room.

"Are you with Allen," Lida asked, "or with one of your other johns?"

Diana giggled again. "Allen missed his plane," she explained.

"Listen," Lida went on, "because this is important. And

236

brace yourself." She winked at Duvivier through the glass partition of the booth. "That friend of Allen's, that Paul Riley? It was Paul Riley—not Ronald Wendolyn—who killed Christine Rivers. And this morning, Paul Riley tried to kill *me*."

"Oh, my God," Diana said. Her voice drifted away, and Allen came on the phone.

"Are you with Wendolyn?" he said sternly.

Lida jerked the phone away from her ear. "Put Diana back on," she said.

"Where are you?" Allen insisted.

"Relax," Lida said. "I'm on the streets of the nation's capital and it's broad daylight." Then she told him the story, from the Howard Johnson's to the Air and Space Museum, pausing at odd intervals to insert more coins. During these stops Allen relayed the tale, piecemeal, to Diana.

"Oh, my God," Diana's faraway voice kept saying.

Now Lida listened. Duvivier watched her until he couldn't take it any longer. He opened the door to the booth. "What's going on?" he said. "You haven't said anything for the last five minutes."

"Shhh," Lida told him. "We're tying up all the loose ends."

"What loose ends?" he asked, watching Lida pocket the remainder of his change.

"The fate of Ronald Wendolyn, for one thing." She looked over at Duvivier. "He'll remain dead, of course. Allen doesn't want to lose his cushy job just yet."

"What cushy job?"

"He holds the Wendolyn Professorship. Perks you wouldn't believe!"

"I know all about them," he said.

They came to the curb and he stretched out his arm to stop her. "We have a red light," he said.

"I wouldn't doubt it," Lida answered. "This is Fourteenth

237

Street. A famous red-light district."

"Surely not." He gestured at the mannequins in the department-store window. "They're such a cold-looking bunch."

"Oh, yes," she said, catching his arm and pulling him toward the revolving door. "Let's go in here and shop, like regular folks."

❦

"Is this one of your haunts?" he asked.

"Garfinckel's? Hell, no. The salesgirls are too snooty. I like salesgirls who snivel." She walked over to the perfume counter, reading along a row of bottles.

"What are you looking for?" He spoke over her shoulder.

"There's this commercial," she said. "'You touch Masumi. Masumi touches you.'" She croaked the words, hoping to sound mysterious.

"I have that," A saleswoman stretched toward them. "Here we are." She proffered a squat bottle, a gold atomizer bobbing at its neck.

Lida reached for it, but Duvivier caught her hand. "No," he said to the clerk. "Thank you, but I like the brand the lady is wearing. I don't think she'll try that."

The woman arched her brows and stared at him. She withdrew the bottle, but held it, awaiting Lida's protest.

"What brand?" Lida said, turning toward him. It couldn't be the spermicide. She had scrubbed her hands. "I'm not wearing any perfume."

"Aren't you?" He sniffed at her hair, her throat. "But you are. You smell of last night. And of me."

The Masumi bottle shattered against the floor, and a thick cloud of scent closed around them. "Oh, God, let's get out of here," Lida shouted. "Quick! Before it touches us!"

He followed Lida to the escalator. They took it two steps at a time, dodging matrons with shopping bags, housewives making certain that their toddlers gripped the handrail. When they got off on the seventh floor, Lida was puffing.

"Hey," she said, feigning collapse, "I thought you were an old man."

"I used to be an old man," he answered, taking her hand and leading her through a maze of crushed-velvet sofas and overstuffed chairs.

They stood at the edge of a partitioned square. It was arranged to simulate a room. Unread magazines and bowls of waxed fruit were set to exaggerate the gleam of the coffee table, the end tables. The pillows along the sofa were plumped just-so. Lida appraised the scene. "Barf," she said.

"Where do you live?" he asked. "I mean, what's it like?"

"Not like this," she said, looking at him.

He walked into the room, pulling at her to follow. He sat in an easy chair, but without ease. He sat like someone in a dentist's waiting room.

"Is this Early American?" she asked, and he laughed, leaning forward and taking hold of her bottom. He patted her backside. "Why don't you fix me a drink," he said, "and I'll take my shoes off and tell you all about my day."

She stooped beside the chair, balancing carefully. "Hey," she whispered, "aren't you afraid the meat loaf will burn?"

"You haven't any ear for dialogue," he told her. "It should be *my* meat loaf. 'Aren't you afraid *my* meat loaf will burn.' Women are very proprietary about the food they prepare."

"Aren't you afraid *my* meat loaf will burn?" she said.

"You still haven't any feel for the line. But it doesn't matter. I've always hated your meat loaf."

"Yeah? How about my mashed potatoes?"

"Those too," he said. "Hate 'em."

"Isn't there anything you like?"

"Your meringue." He stroked her hair. "I just love your meringue."

The clerk, having stood on the periphery straightening his tie and deciding between 'Can I help you?' and 'Something I

239

can show you?' cursed his timing and walked away.

Lida didn't notice. She stood. "Meringue isn't enough," she said.

"I know that."

"Jesus Christ," Lida said. "I may not have an ear for dialogue, but I sure do have some talent for analogies."

60

Gloomily Lida and Duvivier stood at the rail. The choppy surface of the Potomac washed against the concrete below. Slap. Slap. Slap. Across the river, a plane lifted, turned, and merged with the gray sky.

"Do you want to go inside somewhere?" he asked.

"No."

"Aren't you cold?"

"Yeah," she said, "I am. But I'm afraid, I don't know, that when we stop walking, it'll be over."

He said nothing, but watched her. A jogger came toward them, his suit fluorescent in the gloom. "Don't jump," the man huffed, and thumped away. Duvivier began to laugh. He'd been trying not to.

"It wasn't that funny," Lida said, looking at him. "Hey, what's the matter?"

He was looking at her lips.

She remembered Danielle at Elizabeth Arden. "Oh, God," she said, "am I getting a mustache?"

"You're getting a cold sore," he said.

"I am not. I've never had a cold sore."

"You're getting one now. Here . . ." He led her toward a parked car. "Look."

They stooped, side by side. Lida turned her head this way and that, examining her reflection.

"See?" he said.

"God damn!" She poked at it with her finger. "It *better* be a cold sore." Then she turned and leaned against the fender of the car. "Does this mean you won't kiss me good-bye?"

He held her shoulders and kissed her, kissed her, kissed her, catching her lips with his, her tongue with his, sticky, inside-out kisses.

"This is a disgusting display," she said when she could. "Let's go back to your hotel."

"I will," he said, "but only for my suitcase. Beyond that, I don't have a hotel, remember? I've checked out." Kissing her eyelids, her cheeks, small wet kisses that made her skin blaze cold in the wind. "Lida," he said, "I'll confess."

She pulled away and looked at him seriously.

"I've always hated cute noses," he said, sucking at the tip of hers. "I'm so glad you don't have one." He cupped her face with his hands and blew a little stream of breath back and forth across her lips.

"What are you doing?" she asked.

"Don't you know?"

"No."

"I'm healing you," he said, blowing softly.

Healed, she thought. That would mean walking away. The way that cats do. They lick at each other, rub a bit, and then they walk away.

"What are you thinking about now?" he asked.

"About one of those trick tests. You know. Pseudo-psychology?"

His eyes said he didn't know. "My friend Diana," she explained, "asked me once what I would be if I could transmute."

"And you said?"

"A cat."

"I would be one of my heroes," he told her.

"That's just it. It turned out that they had given this test to incoming freshmen. The A's wanted to be people. You're an A, you see."

"And the B's?"

"I don't know about the B's, but the C's wanted to be animals. I'm a C, that's all. Just a C."

He laughed.

"It gets worse," she said.

"How can it get worse?"

"I really wanted to be a Grecian urn. I didn't say it because I thought it sounded corny."

"Where would that put you?"

"In with the remedials. They wanted to be inanimate objects."

Two taxis pulled to the curb beside them, as if on cue. She and Duvivier stopped walking.

"And what are you thinking?"

"About the Grecian urn," he said.

They stood on the sidewalk, their collars upturned, their hands in their pockets.

"All this snappy patter," Lida said, "it's a habit."

"Yes. It's called persiflage. We're awfully good at it, both of us."

They both turned to look at the taxis. Like vultures, Lida thought, idling there.

"Right now," she asked, "just like this?"

"Yes, I think so." He walked toward the first cab.

Lida, catlike, moved toward the second.

Duvivier stopped, his hand resting on the door handle. "Lida," he called, "you aren't going to get in that thing and shout 'Follow that cab!' are you?"

Lida shook her head. "No."

"Good." He took his seat. She saw him lean forward to speak to the driver. Then he turned and looked at her through the back window. But only for a moment.

✿

"What if she don't?" the driver asked Duvivier.

"Then we'll go back. Keep watching."

"But you'll pay me for the trip to the airport, right? No matter what?"

"Yes. Keep watching."

✿

She imagined him boarding the plane, a Margaux Hemingway stewardess beaming down at him, checking his name on the passenger list, putting a star beside it in the margin. And later she would slither up the aisle, thrust her bosom in his face, and simper, "Coffee? Tea? Or me?"

Lida saw him there in his seat, initially perplexed. His eyes would travel slowly up, up, up. He would look her in the eye, smile deliciously. He would lean back and give her his answer. "Coffee," he would say.

Or would he?

"Hey, lady," her taxi driver said, opening his door and getting out. "What is this? Are ya comin' or what?"

Lida thought of her list. Of the seamy slot for her thirty-fourth lover. "Yeah," she told the driver, easing inside. And then her voice came loud, far from a purr. "Yeah," she said. "Just follow that cab."

244